By the same author

DEATH IN THE OLD COUNTRY

SMOKE DETECTOR

THE NIGHT THE GODS SMILED

The Man Who Changed His Name

The Man Who Changed His Name

An Inspector Charlie Salter Mystery

Eric Wright

CHARLES SCRIBNER'S SONS / NEW YORK

Library of Congress Cataloging-in-Publication Data

Wright, Eric.
The man who changed his name.

I. Title.
PR9199.3.W66M34 1986 813'.54 85-25080
ISBN 0-684-18635-7

Composition by Maryland Linotype, Baltimore, Maryland
Manufactured by Fairfield Graphics, Fairfield, Pennsylvania
Designed by Susan Lu

First American Edition

For Bella Pomer

The Man Who Changed His Name

Chapter

1

"What's she like now?"

"Older. Pretty grungy-looking clothes. You know. Not much flash."

Charlie Salter and his wife were drinking coffee after dinner and discussing the sudden reappearance, that morning, of Salter's first wife after twenty-five years.

"What did she want?" Annie had already asked this question but had obviously not listened to Salter's answer.

He explained again. "She was making inquiries about a friend who was murdered last October."

"Why you? You're not in Homicide," Annie said, indicating what her previous question really meant.

Salter shrugged. The answer was obvious enough: because he was the only cop she knew, even after twenty-five years. And just maybe she was taking the opportunity to get a look at him again, which was the possibility in Annie's head. Not that Annie felt threatened, of course, just a trifle edgy when old wives she had never met popped out of closets.

"When do you see her again?" Annie asked.

"In a few days. When I've talked to Harry Wycke and found out what she wants to know."

It was too soon for all the interesting questions, like how did Salter feel about her now, and did he still see why he had married her in the first place, so Annie stayed silent, waiting for the ghost to leave.

Gerry had appeared that morning when Salter was sitting at his desk making up the Christmas lists. There were nineteen shopping days left. Somewhere up in the high Arctic, winter was organizing itself for a descent on Toronto, but on December 3 the city was still hanging on to the last few exquisite fragments of the longest autumn anyone could remember.

He looked at the general list and began to make a little sublist of kinds and quantities of liquor. Which liqueur was "in" this year? Last year it was Sambuca; the year before, Amaretto. Annie would know. Salter felt proud of himself. He had been thoroughly systematic. Christmas was approaching, season of hope, anxiety, stress, and suicide; for once he was ahead of the game.

Sergeant Gatenby, his assistant, put his head round the door. "There's a lady to see you," he said. "She doesn't have an appointment."

"What does she want?"

"She says she's an old friend."

"What's her name?"

Gatenby's head disappeared and reappeared after a brief pause.

"Miss—sorry, Mzzzz Wellman."

"Never heard of her. All right, send her in." He put the lists into a drawer and waited.

The clothes of the woman who came through the door fitted exactly the term nondescript: blue quilted parka, faded brown jean-type trousers, and scarred boots. She looked like a housewife dressed to clean out an unheated garage.

"Hello, Charlie," she said.

Salter stared at her hard. Her face was shockingly familiar, like that of a well-known actress encountered on a street, but it took him an insultingly long time to make sense of the familiar features. Her identity reached his brain just in time to validate the pleased look of recognition he had stuffed into his own features while he waited.

"Gerry," he said. "What's this Wellman bit?"

"My name, Charlie. I married again."

Where to start? Salter went around the desk to shake hands with his first wife. She accepted his hand, then kissed him quickly and firmly on the lips. Salter tried to translate this gesture while he placed a chair for her and returned to his own. It was positive, indicating that as far as she was concerned there was no hostility. It was also very slightly aggressive, as in the old days. He wondered how much of his own emotional chaos was showing.

"I thought you would be a deputy chief by now," she said, looking round Salter's not very distinguished office and unzipping her parka. "Can I take this off?"

Salter came round the desk again and hung up her coat, grateful for something to do. "So did I," he said. He sat down and looked at her. What did she want? No makeup, washday hands, but she had kept her figure and most of her looks. It must be personal, he thought, but she had no claim on him, none at all. Was she ill? Or broke? Not obviously either. "Want some coffee?" he asked.

"Yes, please. Can I smoke? You never started, did you?"

"No." Salter gave her an ashtray and went to the door to get his sergeant to bring them some coffee, ignoring the look of inquiry on Gatenby's face. While they waited for the coffee, Salter suppressed the urge to speak. His chest was still banging unpleasantly, and he forced himself to sit still.

"You look well," she said. "You haven't changed much, really. Did you get married again?"

"Yes, I did. Eighteen years ago." Why did she want to know? Every sentence was in danger of being deformed by the emotional difficulty of coping with the real situation while trying to frame the platitudes of an ordinary encounter. He could think only of her face, which had again become that of the girl he had left twenty-five years ago: narrow, bladelike, with not enough gap between the eyes, and a long nose, but with a delicate, pretty mouth and a nice complexion that always seemed slightly tanned. Striking is what they used to call her, he thought, and striking she still was.

"Yes," Salter said, registering that she had asked him a question. "Two boys, eleven and fourteen."

"Don't you have a picture of your wife on your desk?"

What the hell was going on? She was acting as if they had bumped into each other on the subway. When was she going to get to the point? "No," he said. "I've never got around to it," and felt pleased that she would have to remain that much in the dark about him.

"What's she like, your wife?"

Salter, slightly paranoiac, thought he detected a tiny note of patronage in her voice, a small maternal note; he thought he heard her asking if he had this time managed to find someone more doting than his first wife, a nice little girl that he could manage. The question was unanswerable anyway. "She's lost all her teeth and one eye is a bit higher than the other," he said. "But she's got a wonderful personality."

"All right, Charlie, all right. I was only asking."

"What the hell do you expect me to say? She's more beautiful than you are? Ugly, but wonderful in bed? A great cook? All of the above?" It was a relief to be able to be rude.

The arrival of Gatenby with the coffee interrupted them. Again, the sergeant made a conspirator's face at Salter, which he ignored.

She took a sip of coffee and started again. "I'm just trying to make conversation. I'm nervous. Aren't you?"

It was an appeal, and he tried to respond.

"Why did you come?" he asked. "After twenty-five years it can't be personal. So what's wrong?"

"I'd like some help. It *is* personal, though. I could have come to anyone, but I thought I'd take the opportunity to see you again. I was your virgin bride once, and I still feel a bit connected to you."

"You made a mistake and so did I. We went through all that," Salter said, thus announcing that it was time to get on with it, that whatever lay between them in the past was not worth anymore chat.

She looked for a moment as if she was going to challenge Salter's right to close down the conversation, but then, after a few moments, she straightened herself in her chair. "Still hostile after all these years," she said. "Maybe that's better than not feeling anything."

"Yeah, maybe I should work on it. Get in touch with my hostility. Let it all hang out, eh?"

She laughed. "You're mixing up your terms, Charlie."

"Good. Now. What can I do for you?"

"A woman was murdered two months ago and you guys don't give a goddamn about it."

Salter put down his pen and sat back. "If you want any help from me you'll have to change your tone," he said. "If you just want to call the police names, I'll send you down to Homicide."

They looked at each other for a few moments, squaring for a contest. "Now. What can I do for you?" Salter repeated. "I'm not in Homicide."

"I know that. I've been checking up on you. I thought you might be able to tell me what you've done, or what

Homicide has done, I suppose. Find out why no arrests are imminent, as they say. Find out if anyone gives a damn when a woman is raped and murdered around here, as opposed to caring so much if someone walks up and down outside the U.S. Consulate with a sign."

"Here we go again," Salter said. This had been their point of departure twenty-five years ago. Newly married to a young policeman, she had been caught up almost immediately by the social upheavals that flowered in the sixties. Marijuana had appeared, an interesting new experience for her, illegal and potentially career-destroying for him. Then the politics began. Salter had always thought of himself as left wing in a working-class way, but he was put off as much by the hysteria of some parts of the new left as he had always been by the trough-swilling antics of the major political parties. In his view Gerry had been undiscriminating, embracing the new, castigating the old. She had forced him to choose, so they had separated and then divorced.

"Well, nothing much has changed, has it?" she said.

Privately Salter was inclined to agree. The nuclear clock was still ticking off the seconds to doomsday, there were no fish left in the lakes, and child pornography had become a very big business. But he didn't want to argue about it. "What do you want me to do?" he asked.

"Just find out if anything is being done about this woman."

"All right." He could ask Wycke, his friend in Homicide. "What's her name?" He pulled a sheet of paper toward him.

"Nancy Cowell. She was found dead, strangled in her apartment."

Salter put down his pen. "The social worker?" he asked.

"That's the one," Gerry said.

"Was she a friend of yours?"

"No. A friend of a friend."

Salter was as familiar with the case as anyone who read the newspapers. The murder of Nancy Cowell had created a sensation two months before. The police had so far failed to find the killer.

"What kind of social work did she do?" Salter asked. "Your kind of stuff?" His attention was still focused almost wholly on Gerry.

"What kind of stuff do I do, Charlie?"

"Let me think. Organizing single parents' associations. Demonstrations against rent increases. Stuff like that." Salter smiled, hoping for a response that would soften the strain a little.

She shook her head, then smiled very slightly in return. "No, she was a professional. I'm not. I'm still what the professionals call a do-gooder. Nancy Cowell dealt mostly with first-time offenders, helping them when they got out of prison."

"Do you know much about her personal life? Her social life?"

"Not really. Why?"

"Where did she meet the men she knew? Were they all social workers?" If I can keep this up a bit longer, thought Salter, I'll soon get used to having her in the room.

"I don't know. You're going to have to ask my friend Agnes about things like that."

"I'm not going to ask anyone about anything, except Homicide, so I can tell you what's happening on the case—if they'll tell me. What I mean is, do you know if she went to singles bars, places like that?"

"I don't know. What difference does it make? She's still dead."

"But you can see why we might have had a problem. Cases involving lonely women are high on the unsolved list. I'll ask, though."

Surprisingly, she didn't debate the point. "I know," she said. "Given the number of weirdos there are about, some women take some awful chances."

"You take a chance every time you step out of the house."

"Men and women both. The risk I'm talking about is being raped at knifepoint. When did that last happen to any of your pals?"

"I'll ask Homicide," Salter said again. He wondered if she had paid as little attention to the content of their conversation as he had. For him, the ostensible subject of Nancy Cowell had got him over the shock of seeing Gerry again, and now he felt he could manage a genuine conversation, an exchange of personal information, as with an old acquaintance.

"How are you?" he asked.

She laughed. "Didn't you say that already? I guess not. I'm fine. I work for the city. I'm a community organizer, paid by the taxpayer, like you. Appointed by the mayor himself, bless his little heart. It pays enough for one to live on."

That figured. Her clothes, while not spelling activist, nevertheless had nothing to do with traditional female careers.

"You live alone?" he asked. Then, "Sorry. It's none of my business."

"Oh, I think you're entitled. No, I live with my sixteen-year-old son. I got married again, and divorced again—I won't tell you why, you might say I told you so—but I kept his name because that's his son's name."

"Finished with men, have you?" Salter was getting comfortable enough to tease a little.

"Nearly. I'm trying to give them up. It's easier than giving up smoking. But I don't hate them, if that's what you mean. There are one or two decent guys around."

"And the boy?"

She made a wry face. "He disapproves of me a bit, but we get along for these days. Guess what he wants to do?"

Salter shrugged and thought of the thing she would like least. "Corporation lawyer?" he hazarded.

"Nearly. He wants to join the Mounties."

Salter laughed. "Can't you talk him out of it?"

"Why should I? I figure it's in his genetic makeup, like they say about criminals nowadays. There must be cops in my background—apart from you, I mean. When can I come back?"

"Give me a few days. I know a guy in Homicide and I'll make a casual inquiry the next time I see him. I'm not the person you ought to be asking, you know. If you want to push it, you can go see Homicide yourself."

"What *do* you do, Charlie? They told me you were in General Duties. What does that mean?" She looked round his office, trying to read the signs, but there were very few to help her: a single filing cabinet, an almost bare desk, an old newspaper picture of Sergeant Gatenby saluting a royal duke, taped to the wall.

"When you arrived I was making up my Christmas list," Salter said.

"And when you're not doing that?"

"I work on special assignments."

"A dogsbody?"

"At one time, about a year ago, yes. But it's getting better. I had a bit of luck and the superintendent I work for decided to hang on to me. *He* gets all the special jobs. And that's all you need to know," he said, slightly tender about the near accuracy of her description.

"Well, it's nice to see you again. It really is. You haven't changed much."

"Nor have you," he said, and then, because it sounded like a crack, "I'm glad you came in."

"So am I." She waited for something else from him. When nothing came, she stood up and rummaged in the pocket of her coat and brought out a notebook. "Here's my office number." She handed him a card. "Here, I'll write my home number on the back." She smiled at him. "I told Agnes I didn't think you were as bad as the rest of them." She waved her hand to include the Metro police force.

"Yes, I am," Salter said. "Pure fascist pig and proud of it. And *you* are using your influence with the establishment." He helped her into her parka.

She took her time zipping up her coat and adjusting her gloves, as if she were trying to find some words to acknowledge the vibrations generated by the meeting of two old lovers. Salter waited for her to speak, but in the end she merely touched his arm and left.

He went back to his desk and tried to return to his Christmas lists, but Gerry had brought back a past he thought he had successfully suppressed. They had married in 1959 when Salter was just twenty-two, newly inducted as a constable in the police force. Gerry was a year older, a recent graduate of the University of Toronto, where she had majored in art and archaeology. They had come from different worlds and met at a picnic on Ward's Island organized by friends of hers, a picnic to which he had been invited by the couple who owned his rooming house. The sixties were just beginning to stir to life. Salter's rooming house was more casually run than it would have been even five years before, and all the tenants were young, like the owners. Later, after Salter left it, it was to become more communal still, until finally the owners sold it to a therapy group, who had made the final transition to a commune.

But this was in the future. When Salter met Gerry, he was struck with her in the traditional way and courted her accordingly. For her part, she had been eager to embrace the young Salter, intrigued at the idea of marrying a policeman, and after three months of summer courtship they were joined at a small ceremony in the island's church. Almost immediately, she became an explorer of the new exploding society, dragging him unwillingly into it, beginning with parties where the men no longer wore ties and the prevailing smell was of incense. Marijuana arrived, and Salter became more disturbed as it became necessary for her to join the new communion. One night Salter, sipping beer in the kitchen of an old house in the Annex, realized that he was sitting across the room from an undercover cop from the drug squad. He went in search of Gerry and dragged her from the party. They made their way home, walking four feet apart, shouting at each other.

For a few more months they limped along, but Gerry was now right in the middle of the new scene and began to question his "role" in the oppression of society. They endured a curious period, socially completely at odds, but liking each other still, and still making love. Then, without (as far as he knew) being unfaithful, she told him she found monogamy restricting and demeaning. They separated then, and divorced as soon as they could.

He had seen her on the news several times since, sitting down outside Parliament, lying down outside bomb factories, marching, protesting. No one in the police department knew they had once been linked—the information was no longer important—but why had he never said anything to Annie when Gerry appeared on the screen? "I married a hippie" was his story, and "I haven't seen her for twenty years." Now the thing had happened that he had always slightly feared. She was back to embarrass him, but not in the way he said she used to. She was not the screaming feminist/hippie/outsider that he had created over the years, but someone who looked more or less normal. Now, he thought, she might set Annie to wondering what it was, not about her but about Salter, that had made the marriage impossible all those years ago. Annie, he thought, might like her.

Pondering all this, Salter was visited by the awareness, not of the dark times, but of why he had married her in the first place. The change in her looks was not so great as it might have been, and she had retained, it seemed to him, the same air of curiosity that had once focused on him and made him feel interesting, the curiosity that had made her want to experience each new phenomenon the rapidly shifting age offered. Today, thought Salter, we would have had an affair and lived together for six months, and she would have moved on. We would probably have stayed on good terms.

On the way home he considered how he would tell

his wife about his visitor. "Guess who turned up today?" seemed safest. He had always cut discussions of his first wife to a minimum. What was Annie's reaction likely to be?

Her car was parked in the street. With any luck she would be in the kitchen covered with flour, which was how Salter liked to find her. Her job in an advertising agency kept her late without warning sometimes, and Salter had still not got over the feeling, when he came home first and found the house empty, that he would never see her again, that he would be met with a note saying, "I can't stand it any longer. Do not try to find me. One day I will try to explain."

But she was in the kitchen stirring a big pot of chili, and Salter kissed her with more care than usual and got a pat in return.

"Got some news for you," she said, when he was in his stocking feet with a beer in his hand, sifting through the day's mail.

"What's that?" he asked, not wanting to know. Basement full of water? Son broken a leg? Wife going to Nevada for six weeks to shoot a commercial?

"Mother and Dad are coming for Christmas."

Not bad, but not good, either. "When did that happen?"

Mother and Dad were Annie's parents, the Montagus, who kept a grand home on Prince Edward Island, where they were part of the gentry.

"Today. Mother called and said they would be alone, so I invited them. They've wanted to come for years."

"What's with Bill and Donald?"

Annie's brothers, both married, also lived on the Island, and the clan usually gathered at one of the houses over the holidays.

"They're both going to the girls' families this year. Mother and Dad were invited, of course, but it seemed like a good year for them to come to us." Annie spooned the chili into bowls, called their sons, Angus and Seth, to dinner, and got the toast from the oven where it had been keeping warm.

Salter took a tentative spoonful and asked, delicately, keeping any bias out of his voice, "Are they staying here?"

"No, at the Benvenuto," Annie said, naming a swank hotel on Avenue Road. "They'll go back to the hotel each night."

That was something. Now that his own father had a girl friend, he would also go home at night, leaving the Salters with a chance to breathe between rounds.

"You think they'll get along?" he asked, meaning the two sets of parents.

"Dad can get along with anyone," Annie said. "And May will just sit in the corner as usual." May was Salter's father's girl friend, the self-effacing widow of one of his father's former workmates.

"Which leaves Mother and my dad," Salter said, noting to himself that "Dad" was "Dad" at any level, but as you moved up the class ladder in Canada, "Mum" became "Mother." Or maybe it wasn't a class thing. Maybe, as a taxi driver in New York had explained to him, Canada, like America, didn't have a class structure. "We don't have different classes here, like the Brits," the cab driver had explained. "Just different elements of society."

"They'll manage," Annie said. "And so will we."

"So long as your mother doesn't start quoting poetry," Salter said.

Annie said nothing. Annie's father was a doctor-turned-businessman; the old man was courteous, kind and generous to the boys, and very easy to be with. Annie's mother was more of a problem because she was incapable of realizing that she could ever give offense. She, too, came from old Island money, but before she married she had served briefly as an English teacher in the days when high-school students memorized poetry for marks, and she had a head full of verse to suit any occasion. Once, when he shouted at the boys at the dinner table, telling them to shut up, Mrs. Montagu murmured, "He gave commands, all smiles stopped therefore," one of the few bits of poetry that Salter was familiar with. After that, he was never sure when she quoted verse that he was not being put down in iambs. Nevertheless he had learned in the eighteen years he had known them to be fond of them both, and now that he was reaching the age of sentiment he liked more and more the idea of bringing the whole family together for a festive occasion.

The real problem, as both he and Annie knew, was Salter's father. The old man was a retired maintenance man with the Toronto Transit Commission. He was manageable on his own, or rather accompanied by his silent girl friend, but he might be hard work at the same table as the Montagus. His father's back was permanently up, and he would be on the watch for the smallest slight, the tiniest hint of patronage from Annie or her parents that he could take offense at and turn into a grievance. But there was nothing to be done about it. Salter's father always ate Christmas dinner with his only child, and the Montagus could not be put off any longer.

Salter took his coffee over to an armchair and waited for his two sons, who had been listening with ears like bats to the problems of family relations in an adult world, to leave him and Annie alone. When the boys gave up hope of hearing anything more and moved upstairs to study, he casually introduced the subject of his visitor.

Now Salter took advantage of Annie's silence and changed the subject back to Christmas. "What will it consist of?" he asked. "Will we have to feed them on Christmas Eve, all day Christmas, and Boxing Day, too? Jesus."

"They don't have anyone else to visit in Toronto, but Dad said he wants to take us all out for dinner on Boxing Day."

"My dad, too? He won't come. You know him."

"We'll ask him, and he can do what he likes."

"Christmas Day could be a long one," Salter said.

"Oh, don't let's plan on having a difficult day before they arrive. Wait and see. It might be all right."

"I'll get Dad, my dad, hammered," Salter said.

"He gets a bit cantankerous when he's been drinking."

"He's a bit cantankerous when he's sober, but in a different way to when he's pissed. But you're right. Let's keep our fingers crossed and hope for the best."

Thus Gerry was disposed of—for the moment, anyway.

Chapter

2

Harry Wycke was the closest person to a friend that Salter had in Homicide, or anywhere else in the force, and the next morning he found the time to seek out Wycke in his office. He introduced the topic carefully, an informal, casual query to satisfy his obligation to an old acquaintance.

"Who is this woman?" Wycke asked immediately.

"She works out of the mayor's office. Some kind of community organizer."

"I haven't heard from his worship. Why doesn't she ask him to ask me? Why you?"

Yes. Why doesn't she ask the mayor? Because she wanted to get a look at Salter again? Right.

"I was married to her once," Salter said, and looked out the window.

"Were you, by Christ! I didn't know you had a past. Have the Mounties got you in her file?"

"Probably. It happened twenty-five years ago. It was a mistake."

"But now she's back, asking you for favors?"

"That's what it looks like. She may be just using me as a friend at court. But she left me or I left her because of the way she felt about cops. I don't want to fob her off. I'd like to show her that we *do* give a shit about murdered women."

"Send her over to Public Relations."

"Then she would be right, wouldn't she? Could you just look it up for me?"

"Sure; I don't have to. I know the case. We're still working on it. But don't take on the honor of the force all by yourself, pal. Leave that to the chief."

"When can I come back? When will you have had time to check it?"

Wycke looked irritated. "Let's do it now. I've got nothing better to do." He looked around at the piles of paperwork on his desk.

Salter swallowed the irony. "Thanks."

Wycke led him along a corridor and down some stairs to the office of a sergeant in plain clothes, a yellow-haired man with dark jowls and the raw nose of someone nursing a heavy cold.

"Sergeant Marinelli," Wycke said to Salter, and then to the sergeant, "This is Inspector Salter, works for Orliff. He's been asked for a status report on the Cowell case. You remember, Nancy Cowell? Probably some politico's girl friend."

"Why didn't they ask us?" Marinelli said, taking a deep sniff and not moving.

Salter stayed mute. Wycke said, "I already said that, Stan. He doesn't know."

Marinelli sniffed again, looking now at Salter. "There's no status on the case," he said. "We've run out of leads. You got a fresh one?"

"Can you tell me what you've done so far?" Salter began, but Wycke laid a hand on his arm.

"The inspector needs a brief resumé," he said. "But a full one. Otherwise whoever is interested will keep coming back asking if we've done this or that. You know. Let's blind them with bullshit and they'll go away."

"It ain't bullshit," Marinelli said. "We've done everything." He pulled some Kleenex out of a box and wiped his upper lip. When he was satisfied that he could safely move away from the tissues for a few seconds he walked over to a file cabinet and pulled out a folder about three inches thick. "You want to read it, or shall I take you through it? This is where it starts." The drawer was full of similar folders.

"If you've got the time, I'd be grateful," Salter said.

The sergeant arranged himself at his desk and indicated a chair where Salter could sit beside the desk and take notes.

"I'll leave you guys," Wycke said. "Thanks, Stan. Call in before you go, Charlie."

"You want something to write on?" Marinelli asked,

pushing a sheet of paper over to Salter. "Right. Here goes. Nancy Cowell, found dead at eight-thirty A.M. October eighth. Strangled and evidence of intercourse."

"Raped?"

"We don't know. It doesn't always leave signs, you know. There were signs of a struggle and there was semen, but there were no signs of abuse anywhere else on the body, except that she'd been strangled. She was known to be alive at eleven-thirty, when she called a friend."

"Who found her?"

"Her friend. The one she phoned. Agnes Loomis, a community worker. The two of them had arranged to go to the St. Lawrence market that morning and Loomis was waiting outside the apartment block in her car. When Cowell didn't show, Loomis got the super to let her in to wake her up. They found her on the floor, still in her nightgown and bathrobe."

"What do you know about her?"

"She was a social worker, from Winnipeg. She left her husband and had been living in Toronto for six months. She worked with first-time offenders, guys trying to stay out of jail." Marinelli paused and looked significantly at Salter.

"So one of them called on her late at night, persuaded her to let him in and killed her," Salter said obediently.

Marinelli nodded approval of Salter's surmise. "Right," he said. "That's what *we* thought, too. But we checked them all, I mean *really* checked them—" Marinelli's impersonation of his favorite television sergeant was interrupted by several sneezes and a lot of mopping. When he resumed, his voice was matter-of-fact. "We even checked on their pals—anyone who might have known that she lived there alone, but we were satisfied that none of them knew where she lived. She never gave out that information on principle." Marinelli looked down at the file for his place. "The next thing was to check on any other male contacts she had. There was no regular boyfriend, but Loomis put us on to the fact that she was trying to meet men. She had tried a few singles bars, and some outfit called the Get-Together Club where a bunch of lonely hearts meet, and she put an ad in the paper."

"Christ," Salter said, acknowledging the size of the search Marinelli and his men had had to make.

"Right," the sergeant said. "We checked every singles bar in town, over and over again. We found a couple of people who thought they had seen her a while ago, but no one who could connect her with anybody. This Get-Together thing was a washout, too. We did find someone who remembered her going to a meeting three months ago, but she only stayed a little while."

"But if it was someone there, or at a bar, the only one who would remember, probably, was the guy who picked her up."

"Right. She didn't go to these places with a girl friend."

"What about the ad?"

Marinelli held up a sheaf of papers. "She got thirty-two replies, and she answered five of them."

"How do you know?"

"She listed them all. Very methodical. We checked every one just in case, but all except the five said they hadn't heard from her, and that checks with what she wrote on their letters. As for the last five, two of them were out of town, two others have alibis and we think they're clean, and the last one we haven't been able to find yet."

"Disappeared?"

"Nah. He didn't write his address on the letter, and we can't read his signature. He enclosed a card with his name and address but we can't find the card."

"Can I see those letters?"

"Sure. I'll get you copies of them, so you can read them in peace without catching this goddamn cold." Marinelli yelled through the door and a constable came in and got orders to run off copies of the letters.

Marinelli continued. "We know she had dinner with someone that night—she told Loomis when she called her—and if it was a girl friend we figured she would have come forward by now, but no one has, so we checked just about every restaurant in town. No dice. No one remembered seeing her. Finally I had a team working the area she lived in—you remember how we caught that magazine salesman in the West End? We did a canvass, questioned everybody in the area, hundreds of them, some of them three or four times. Nothing. No one remembers anyone wandering around that night, though that's not surprising. It was a hell of a night, pissing down until about four A.M. We're now trying to think what to do next. Got any suggestions?"

Salter shook his head. "Her husband?"

Marinelli riffled through the file and took out a sheet of paper. "Lives in Winnipeg. That weekend he was closing up his cottage in Rat Portage, about a hundred and thirty miles away." Marinelli paused. "Rat Portage?" he repeated. "That's a hell of a name. Can that be right?"

Salter nodded. "I know it," he said. "It's near Kenora. I spent a summer there once."

"Yeah?" Marinelli waited politely for a reminiscence, then continued. "He left his mother's house in the North End of Winnipeg on Friday evening and drove to his cottage, coming back on Sunday. He was seen at the cottage on Sunday morning, but no one noticed him before that. He *could* have caught a plane on Friday night and flown back on Saturday. So you know what we did, just in case? We checked the passenger lists—he wasn't on them—then we checked all the passengers we could find, everybody except one man and one woman. He had to sit next to somebody, but no one remembered him."

"Did she have an address book?"

"Yes, she had an address book, and we checked it out. Except for the Winnipeg numbers, there were about a dozen that were real people, and not, you know, her dentist and stuff. One of them was Agnes Loomis, the woman who found her, and three others were girl friends. Two were guys who had left town long before, and all the others checked out with solid stories."

The patrolman returned with the copies of the letters and Marinelli gave them to Salter. "Okay?" he said. "Now you can tell them we haven't been sitting on our asses."

"I'll tell them. Thanks."

"You're welcome. And if anything occurs to you that we haven't done, let me know first, will you?"

"It doesn't look very likely, but I'll tell Inspector Wycke if I see anything."

"Good." Marinelli went back to cleaning up the damage from another sneeze, and Salter left.

When he went back up the stairs to Wycke's office, Wycke was just putting the phone down. "That was Marinelli," he said. "Wants to know if he can trust you. I told him yes. He said he'd heard you were a good person to stay away from on account of the boys upstairs don't like you. I told him about that, too."

"Thanks. He seems to have done a job on this case."

"Will she be satisfied? Your ex?"

Salter shrugged. "*I* am," he said. "Let her go see the mayor if she isn't."

"Ataboy. By the way, you want to buy a cottage?" Wycke spoke lightly, ready to pretend he was kidding.

"Yours?" Salter asked. "You wouldn't sell that, would you?" The cottage was a cabin on the Pickerel River, a fishing camp Salter had borrowed once and lusted after ever since.

Wycke said, "I never get up to it, and I can't keep it

up. It needs looking after. How about it?" He was serious now, pressingly slightly.

But Salter shook his head. "My kid didn't like fishing. Hang on for another ten years and I'll buy it for my retirement."

Wycke made a face. "It'll disappear back into the bush by then," he said.

"Your father phoned," Annie said after supper that night. "I told him my parents were coming and he said he wouldn't, then, this year."

"What's he going to do instead?" Salter asked, accepting the information temporarily at its face value.

"He said he and May will just stay home and watch TV."

"Why?"

Annie shook her head and shrugged her shoulders, an it's-*your*-father gesture.

"Because we didn't invite him earlier, do you think?" Salter asked.

"Could be. I said we had invited my folks and that he and May would enjoy meeting them and he said not to bother, he wasn't sure we were having anything this year because he hadn't heard from us, so he and May decided to stay home."

"We've offended him, then. When did he expect us to let him know that this year, like every year for the last ten, he was welcome to join the family feast? Now I'll have to call in, I suppose, and plead with him."

"Maybe he doesn't want to come," Annie said, a rare sign from her that the continual effort to accept cheerfully the burden of keeping Salter's father happy was a strain. The old man was suspicious of Annie's life-style, and she had to tread a delicate line to avoid seeming, on the one hand, to put him down, and on the other, to patronize him by acting to create a common ground. If she served beef bourguignon when he came to dinner she risked his regarding it as one of those bloody Italian concoctions full of garlic, a waste of good food; if she called it "stew" he took it as an attempt to feed him on the cheap with a dish his own wife had made only when they were short of money. Nowadays she served him roast beef, summer and winter, and he made jokes about the fact that it was all the Salters ever ate.

"Of course he wants to come," Salter snapped. "We can't leave them by themselves on Christmas Day, can we? He just wants to be asked properly."

Both of them were silent for a few minutes.

"He won't come out with your folks on Boxing Day," Salter said. Salter's father ate out only at Honest Ed's Warehouse, an establishment without pretense that served Sunday dinner seven days a week in a gala atmosphere.

Annie said quickly, "But *we* are going, Charlie." There were limits to what she would do in the interests of intrafamily harmony, and denying herself dinner at Scaramouche was outside those limits.

Salter considered. Nerves were now slightly on edge,

and he was grateful for Annie's patience with her in-law. "Tell your parents not to invite him and May, and not to mention it," he suggested.

"We can't do that. It'll probably slip out." She rolled her eyes toward Seth, who was watching television. "No, let Dad invite them. They won't come, and if they do, fine."

"He won't come," Salter said.

"Charlie," Annie said, "I am not going to spend the time between now and Christmas worrying if people will get along with each other. I'm looking forward to Mother and Dad being here and I intend to have a good time and try to make sure everybody else does, too. I'll even cook two kinds of stuffing—the one I like, and sage and onion for you and your father. Now, what's on television?"

That's the spirit, thought Salter. Eat, drink, and screw the human factor. She's right. If we start drinking early enough it might work.

"Harry Wycke wants to sell his cottage," he said, changing the subject. "I told him, hang on for another ten years and I'll buy it."

"Maybe Seth will like fishing," she said, acknowledging his regret that neither she nor Angus did.

"He's my last hope," Salter said.

Two days later Gerry turned up in his office, and he told her the results of his inquiries.

"So?" she asked, when he had explained the scope of the investigation.

"So the case is still open, but they have no more leads."

"So nothing more will happen, will it?"

Salter explained the procedure with an open file. "They go through them regularly, trying to find something they've missed. A new guy will come along and spend his spare time reading them. Sometimes they see a new lead to follow, or they get a tip while they're on another case, or someone remembers a face. The case isn't dead."

"It might as well be. How often do you solve a case after two months?"

"I don't know, but it happens. Homicide had a ninety-six-percent success record last year."

She shook herself for action. "I still don't think you guys give a damn about a case like this, especially if she doesn't have anyone going to bat for her. Well, she does now. Me."

"What are you going to do? Hire a private eye?"

"Maybe, but most of all I'm going to make Metro's finest earn their money."

"How?"

"You'll hear," she promised.

"Great. I spend a day getting you information you aren't entitled to. I use up all my personal credit around here because we used to be married. Okay. Now you're going to raise hell, and it'll come right back to this desk. These guys will think I'm doing the shit-disturbing, which is what some of them think I like doing. Don't you think I'm entitled to know what you plan to do so

I can be ready? What's your object? To find this guy or to start a little campaign against the police?"

She had zipped her parka up and was waiting while he finished his speech. Now she sat down. "All right. Here's what I'm going to do next. I work for the mayor. I'll start with him, see what he can do. I know people in the attorney general's office, too. I'll go and see them."

"If they come to us we'll tell them what I told you."

"And if they expect me to accept that, I will tell them what I will do next."

"Which is what?"

She leaned forward in her chair. "Some things *have* changed in the last twenty years, you know. Oh, sure, we still march up and down with signs, organize parades, all that stuff. But we've learned some tricks, too. The Moral Majority isn't the only group that knows how to use the media. Don't you know that there are at least three female columnists in town who make a living writing about injustices to women? Among them they churn out ten or a dozen columns a week. They need material, even when they aren't angry about something themselves. They have to fill a column. Then there's television. What they need, night after night, is stories. Like the newspapers, even if nothing happens they have to get excited about it. How many newscasts, talk shows, sixty-minute probes do you think there are? I can get on enough of them, for long enough, to make damn sure this open file gets an airing."

"You'll lose your job," Salter pointed out.

She laughed. " 'You'll lose your job,' " she intoned. "That'll make about the twentieth time. No, I won't, because that would be news too. Well, maybe in six months. I'll get another. Or go on unemployment. I only took this job because it looked like a chance to get steady wages for doing something useful. I don't worry about jobs, Charlie. I haven't worried about them since I left you. I'm independently poor, and I make out all right. I wasn't planning to make a career of the mayor's office anyway. In a couple of years I want to be doing something more important. Just now, though, I would like to see something happen in this case. Tell me honestly, do you think Nancy Cowell had it coming to her?"

"What?" Salter was appalled. "Murder?"

"Suppose she hadn't been murdered, just raped? I mean, she probably didn't know the guy well and there she is asking him back to her apartment, probably to sleep with him. It's her fault if the guy turns out to be kinky, isn't it?"

"Well, if she doesn't know what she's getting into . . ."

"You're never sure. Lots of women find out after they've *married* that Dr. Jekyll and Mr. Hyde is a true story. But reverse the situation. If a man picks up a woman at a bar, takes her back to his place, and she stabs him while they're making out, then cuts his balls off, you'd look for her very hard, wouldn't you?"

"What is this, Gerry? I thought Nancy Cowell was just an excuse to—well, see me again. Now you're calling me one of 'you guys' who don't give a damn. You asked me to find out something. So I've found out. If you want to follow it up, go ahead. But don't make me the goat. I'm just a guy you used to be married to, remember? We're divorced now, so quit shouting at me. Okay?"

She accepted the reproof with a tight nod, then set it aside. "Just tell me this. If the reverse situation *did* happen, would you, Charlie Salter, really say that it's his fault for taking her home? Women don't commit sex crimes, but according to you they cause them."

"I'm not going to argue with you about it. Men rape, women don't. A basic biological difference. Every man is a bit of a rapist and every woman is a bit of a victim. Okay. I agree. Now let's get back to Cowell."

"It's not biological, it's learned. Men learn to rape. In some societies it's unheard of. It's a social thing."

"For Christ's sake, the theories change every week. Like the ones about treating criminals. If you want to know what I think, I think nobody knows anything worth a pinch of crap about why people are the way they are, and I'm certain nobody knows what to do about it. I'm sick and tired of a lot of psychologists and sociologists and educators mouthing a lot of trendy crap that gets reversed five years later when the next gang comes along." Salter was nearly shouting.

"But our policemen are wonderful, are they? You want to hear a few stories about the morality squad?"

"No, I don't." Salter let out a breath. "We're not supposed to lose our temper," he said. "It's part of the training. Let's not do this again, Gerry. Go see the mayor and start round two, but no arguments, please, or we'll be back where we were twenty-five years ago."

There was a long pause. When Gerry spoke again her voice was back to normal. "You're right," she said. "Anybody listening in would sure as hell know we must have been married once." She smiled. "Okay. I'll try to keep it formal, but I do want to see someone act, and right now as far as I'm concerned, you are in charge." She got up and walked to the door. "It *is* nice to see you again, though. I've often thought about you. It's kept me from believing that all cops are alike."

It was an odd form of apology, and Salter looked for several seconds at the closed door, knowing what he had to do next but needing to wait for several minutes until the mingled odors of anger and intimacy had dissipated. Then he picked up the phone and asked for some time with his boss, Superintendent Orliff.

"Liaison, they're calling it," Orliff said. "Liaison officer."

"What the hell does that mean?" Salter asked, still slightly raw and ready to challenge every new term.

"It means that if someone gets killed in Portugal, say, and the Portuguese cops think the killer has a Toronto connection, then we get the job of helping them. That is, *you* get it." Orliff smiled at his own witty acknowledgment that he never left the office if he could help it.

"But we do that now, don't we? Somebody answers the mail with the foreign stamps, doesn't he?"

"What's the matter with you, Salter? You get into a fight with your wife this morning? Sure we respond, but it's kind of hit or miss. They start with Interpol in Ottawa, who get on to us. If somebody steals the Mona Lisa and ships it to Kapuskasing, say, then they get on to the Art and Fraud squad to watch out for it. But now they think this should be centralized. We need a specialist in liaison work who could show foreigners how to use our system, someone they would know to come to. That will be me, in the first instance, then you. I'll list you with Interpol—Salter, Special Liaison Officer." Orliff smiled again. "It's not my idea, but that's what we're getting into. I don't mind. I haven't got too much longer to go." Orliff looked warmly at the pile of papers that contained the plans for his retirement cottage, one of the many neat piles that ringed his desk.

"What happens when we aren't liaising?"

"Oh, liaising is just *one* of the things they have in mind. This special unit they're setting up would do all kinds of things. It's an experiment."

"So what are we—a branch of General Duties?"

"Oh, no. They want us to be independent, flexible. See, one of the ideas is that we would get special tasks and if we show a permanent need for something we don't have now, then a new unit would be set up. If Community Relations didn't exist, say, they would funnel any community problems to us and if we got too many of them I would recommend setting up a community-relations unit. Then we would forget about it. See? Anything that doesn't fit, we get."

"What are we called?"

"That was a problem. They tried 'Unit,' but we already use that as part of a branch, under a deputy, so they thought we should have a new name."

"What are we then?"

"I told you, 'Center.' The Special Duties Center. Very big everywhere, 'centers' are. Sounds like a think tank, doesn't it? I report to all the deputies but I'm not responsible to any of them. I like it, Salter. We can do what we like provided I keep my nose clean."

And you will do that all right, thought Salter. Orliff had a reputation for an impeccable nose. He had no enemies and very few friends; he threatened nobody while keeping close watch on any threats to himself, a careful man who by choosing to be entirely apolitical in a political organization had advanced without haste but without ever slipping backward. He was Salter's opposite in almost every way, and the two men were getting along very well as Salter learned to trust him.

Orliff squared up the little pile of papers that had to do with the new center. "What did you come to see me about?" he asked. "I interrupted you with this new thing."

Salter told Orliff what had happened in detail, including his own relationship with the principal figure in the story.

"I didn't know you were married before. How long ago?"

"Twenty-five years. It only lasted a year."

Orliff waited for more.

"She was one of the first hippies. She wanted to smoke dope, stuff like that. I had just joined the force."

"Wouldn't matter so much now."

"No, but it would be something else. We were incompatible."

Orliff nodded. "So now she's back raising a little dust. Let her."

"No, sir. I wouldn't have bothered you if that's all it was. She's tough, and she intends to make us do something. My judgment is that you ought to be ready."

"You mean *they* ought to. And *I* ought to be ready for *them*." Orliff pointed to the ceiling, a little lesson. "All right, I'll tell them first. In the meantime, think about this 'center' thing. I want to talk some more about how we handle ourselves without putting anyone's nose out of joint." He nodded to dismiss Salter.

In the middle of the afternoon Orliff called Salter back in. "Good judgment, Salter," he said. "We let them know just in time. The mayor's office and some assistant deputy minister have been talking to the chief. After we talked, he decided not to give the usual response that we've done everything we can, which is true. The chief is very pissed off about it, but we found an answer that will keep us and her out of the headlines for a while."

"What?"

"You."

"What does that mean? What am I supposed to do?"

"Start again. Make this your first assignment in the Special Duties Center. Look into this thing until you're satisfied that everything's been done, then satisfy her. Okay?"

"Is this a joke?"

"No, it isn't. The politicos at the Buildings are upset. Your ex-wife has got teeth, and they don't want to get bitten. They're afraid that someone will start demanding new legislation because the present laws are inadequate to protect women, and on and on and on."

"What about us? Are we upset?"

"Not by her. You've looked at the case. We've done our job. But when politicians start covering their asses, anything can happen. We generally feature in the blame."

Salter thought of something else. "Homicide isn't going to like this," he said. "You set me up like some kind of special investigator and they're going to get very edgy."

"I thought about that. Here's how it will work. Homicide has done its job and has nothing to worry about, except from the politicos, and they're very busy right now, as always, so they're going to ask for my help to get these outside people off their backs. There's a guy in Homicide, Wycke, who you'll work with. You get along with him, don't you?"

"How did you know?"

"He's been running interference for you already." Orliff looked at a note on his desk but explained no further. "So the way it is, you deal with this lady, and the rest of the outside stuff, and Wycke will feed you what you need."

And if I'm lucky, thought Salter, Homicide will get the credit. If I'm not, they will still get the credit for having done a thorough job in the first place. But Orliff would know, and that was his only concern.

"Do I let her in on the whole thing?" Salter asked.

"Use your discretion. Tell her what will convince her. Make her go away."

He telephoned Wycke, and the two men agreed to eat lunch at Dooley's, a bar on Bloor Street. "It's a good place to eat and talk," Wycke said. "Except on Fridays, when some kind of immigrant group meets there and makes a lot of noise."

When Salter arrived, Wycke was already eating. Salter took his advice and ordered the shepherd's pie and the house draft.

"This is going to be fun," Wycke said by way of opening the subject and stating his own attitude to it. "How do you plan to start?"

"By reading the files," Salter said. "I'll come back with you and pick them up."

Wycke shook his head. "I want to go through them first, so I'll know who you're talking about. Then you can have them."

"Okay. After I've read the files, I'll give Gerry a short course in police procedure."

"Gerry?"

"My ex-wife. Geraldine."

"Ah. Fancy name." Wycke finished his pie and waited for Salter to continue.

"Then I'll show her how careful you guys have been. When I get the files from you, I'll read them and then I'll see her. Maybe that will be it."

"You know what civilians are like, Charlie. She'll want to know why we haven't questioned everybody in Toronto, put out a dragnet, called in the Mounties—stuff like that."

"I'll explain what good that will do, and what it would cost, and who puts up the money. She's not a knee-jerk cop-hater, I think; she'll be reasonable."

"I thought she *was*. Liberal, hippie, you're-a-bunch-of-fascist-pigs. She's been involved in a lot of stuff."

This is the best bit of gossip these guys have had for weeks, thought Salter. "I know," he said. "But this time she's just concerned about a woman. She's not a kid."

Wycke put a potato chip in his mouth and chewed slowly. "How do you feel about her now? I mean, when she walked in on you, did you want to kick her out, or anything?"

"No. Nothing like that. I could even see why I married her in the first place."

"Still got something going for her?"

"I mean I always knew why we split up, but I couldn't remember why I married her. I can see it now."

"If she feels the same way, good feelings about you, I mean, she won't be out to nail your ass to the wall, will she?"

"I don't think so. She wants to know who killed Nancy Cowell, that's all."

Wycke said no more, and the two men parted with an arrangement to meet the next day.

In the meantime, Salter decided to take an hour off and begin his Christmas shopping. No snow had fallen yet, and so far he had not zipped the lining into his raincoat, but the Salvation Army was jingling away on the street corners and the crowds in the stores were getting irritable. Salter walked into the Hudson's Bay store and found himself at the perfume counter. He took a piece of paper from his wallet; then, suddenly shy of pronouncing the name out loud—it was something like "Desire" with accents on the *e*'s—he handed the paper over to the girl and said, "That's what I want." It was like buying condoms in the fifties.

"How large?" she asked. Salter resisted the urge to reply in terms of the analogy that was running in his head ("Enormous!"), and said, "How much?"

"We have half an ounce for fifty dollars, three-quarters for seventy dollars and an ounce for ninety. It's all in milliliters, but those are the sizes."

"Seventy dollars' worth," Salter said. "Now bath salts. A big bottle."

"What about this?" she asked, holding up a bottle of bath oil that matched the perfume he had bought.

"A bit small," he said.

"You don't use much, and it comes in a big box," the assistant said.

"I'll take it."

"Do you want them gift wrapped, sir?" she asked, taking his charge card.

"Sure."

While he waited, he strolled over to the candy counter to check the price of chocolates imported from Belgium that he had heard Annie mention. They turned out to be nearly as expensive as the perfume, and Salter veered off to buy some horehound candy, which came in a checkered cloth bag to show its authenticity and cost four dollars. She'll like that, he thought. Remind her of her girlhood in the Maritimes.

Next, after picking up his perfume, he went around the corner to Britnell's, where he bought a fresh copy of *Small Talk at Wreyland,* a favorite book of Annie's that she had lost her copy of, and then, because the book was cheap, he urged the assistant to sell him some more and came out of the store with a little book about life in a Norfolk village, another one about life in an Oxfordshire village, and a third one about pioneer days in Ontario. Done, he thought gleefully, done, done, done. He returned to his office and put everything in a drawer; as he surveyed his offerings he knew that whatever happened to the rest of his holiday, Christmas morning would be all right.

He opened another drawer, took out the list, and carefully crossed off Annie's name. Her major gift had been taken care of three months before when an antiques dealer had shown him a little silver tray that Annie could keep her colored decanters on. His sons were no problem: they both wanted noisemakers, a clarinet for Seth, who was in the school orchestra and showing signs of becoming musical, and a tape deck for Angus, who could not get enough of his kind of music out of the family stereo when Salter was around to switch it off. His father was no problem; whatever they got him the old man would find fault with. Salter put down a big bottle of Johnny Walker Black Label against his father's name. Let him find fault with that. Now there was just the tree, the turkey, and the rest of the liquor to worry about. Gifts for Annie's parents, her relatives, their friends, the cleaning lady—all these were Annie's problem.

Chapter

3

Salter was glad that Wycke wanted to read the files first, needing a few days to clear his own desk. He called Gerry to give her the good news about his assignment, warned her not to expect his response for at least a week, and waited, without much appetite, for a call from Wycke. Four days later he was sitting in front of the first file. There were seven of them, brick-colored folders tied up with red tape, each about three inches thick.

"You can forget about those two guys," Wycke said. "Jensen was back in the Don Mills jail that night and Konig was working as a cleaner in the North General Hospital. He was under someone's eye the whole time. There's a letter from the supervisor in the file, giving us shit for checking up on him at all, not giving him a fair chance. We didn't tell them it was homicide."

"Who did these guys hang around with?"

"We checked the lot as far as we could, but remember

she never gave out her address or phone number to her clients. Besides, she might have had dinner with the guy who killed her."

"Huh?"

"She went out to dinner with *someone*. She called Loomis at eleven-thirty to make that date for the market. We think she might have called while the guy was still there—so as not to make it too late to call Loomis—and he killed her afterward."

"What money did she have around?"

"It wasn't a robbery. She had a hundred bucks in her purse, the weekend's groceries, I would guess, and some jewelry, rings, mostly. Whoever did it wasn't a thief, and that's another reason why we figure the one she had dinner with is someone we'd like to talk to."

"But you can't find him or the restaurant?"

"Loomis gave us the names of all the places she might have been in and we got some from her friends, but we couldn't find anyone who saw her."

"What about these singles bars?"

"We checked fourteen of them in the midtown core. Two of the bartenders thought they remembered her, but not that night."

"How do they work, these bars?" Salter asked. "Are they all—" he searched for the term—"meat markets?"

For this, Salter foresaw, was going to be a problem. Happily married for eighteen years, most of which he had spent in police administration, far from the streets, he knew that the sexual chase, what used to be called the dating game, had been transformed in his absence. Like most men of his kind, he got his information from American television shows like *Cheers,* which he watched for laughs, not for its educational value, assuming that *Cheers* had no more relationship to life in Toronto than *Dallas* had to life in Moose Jaw. In short, Salter was out-of-date.

"Don't let anyone hear you, Charlie. You sound *old.* No, as far as I hear—remember, I'm as old as you are—some of them are meat markets, sure, but not all of them, maybe not most."

"How do they know which is which?"

"Beecroft, one of our brighter Redford-type officers, says the real meat markets have a lineup of guys in sunglasses, standing by the bar, checking the door. You should look at a couple, see for yourself."

"Sure. I'll take Annie."

This time Wycke missed the irony in Salter's voice. "I don't think you would see too many couples your age. A few guys your age, on their own."

"But you checked them anyway."

"Right. Beecroft did it. Said it was the best assignment he'd ever had. Said it was sad to see all those old guys still chasing, though. I think he was needling me a little."

"Fuck him, too. All right, what's this Get-Together place?"

"That's a kind of club that meets once a month, and the idea is to mingle in a big group. The organizers had her application on file, and they think they remember her turning up for one meeting."

"Did Beecroft get to any of the members?"

"No. There didn't seem to be any point unless you could get to everybody, and members can bring guests, who don't have to sign in. And the membership changes all the time. It didn't seem likely we would get anywhere."

"Okay. Now what about these five guys she contacted when they answered her ad?"

"See for yourself. Two of them were out of town. One lives with his sister, and she can vouch for him, and one of them was at work by eleven. He's an editor at a news agency, working nights. I'm a bit suspicious of him—he says he was home watching TV. You ever tried to watch the crap they put out on Fridays? Half the time it's those New York stockbrokers talking figures of speech. You know? 'The market's feeling for a bottom, but it will soon take on a fresh supply of oxygen.' "

"You aren't supposed to stay home on Fridays. But if he was at work by eleven he's no good to us. And you never found the missing man? Why?"

"We had nothing to go on. He didn't put his address on the letter and we can't read his name. But the odds are ten to one against him having anything to do with it. The way I figure it, she put his card in her wallet, went out with him once and it didn't work out, so she threw his card away."

"But she kept the letter."

"She kept all the letters."

"What about the husband?" Salter pointed to the name, Kowalczyk. "How do you pronounce it?"

"Kowal*chuk.* Lives in Winnipeg. He was very upset about her, although they'd been separated for six months. He was at his cottage."

Salter nodded.

"He was seen there on Sunday and someone closed the place up that weekend. Every year before he leaves, Kowalczyk puts shutters on all the windows, empties the waterline, cleans out the cupboards, hauls his dock up on the shore, and puts his boat up at the marina. All this was done, and if Kowalczyk didn't do it, who did?"

Salter turned a page. "Who is this Tranby?"

"An old friend of the husband's and, I guess, of hers. Nothing to do with the case. He acted a little bit as a go-between in the early days of the marriage breakup. He lives in Toronto, and he saw her a couple of times after she came to town. He was very helpful to us in filling in the background. He was in Winnipeg that weekend—he's in real estate in Toronto—and he had lunch with Kowalczyk in Winnipeg on the Friday. He heard the news on Sunday when the Winnipeg police came looking for Kowalczyk, and he stayed a couple of days to be with him. Apparently he went to university with both of them."

"What's this name thing? Did she go back to her maiden name when she left him?"

"No. Tranby explained that. Kowalczyk's family is Ukrainian, and years ago when his elder brother started practicing law he persuaded the whole family to change their name, anglicize it, to help him in business. After his wife left, Kowalczyk or Cowell changed his name back to the Ukrainian again, but none of the rest did. So now you have Victor Kowalczyk, his wife, Nancy Cowell, and Mrs. Cowell, a fine old Ukrainian lady who doesn't speak much English. I'm just guessing. I never interviewed her. Weird, eh?"

Salter looked at the files. "I can't go over all this ground again. Got any fresh suggestions that you haven't already followed up?"

"Read all the files three times. Maybe the answer will come to you in your sleep. Otherwise, no."

Salter flipped open the first folder and found an item they had not mentioned, a button that had been discovered in the initial search of the apartment.

"This button," Salter began.

Wycke laughed, interrupting him. "That's our 'clue,' " he said. "Should lead you straight to the killer. One button, raincoat-type, probably London Fog, possibly torn off in struggle. Fragments of cloth attached."

"I've got a raincoat like that," Salter said.

"So have fifty thousand guys in Toronto. If you do find a new suspect with a button missing, it could help. Otherwise I don't think it's much good. They found it under the edge of the couch, so it might have been there since the last tenant."

"What did Forensic have to say?" Salter asked, picking up a thick report.

"Lots, as usual. Hair, blood group, semen, skin, dust

—you name it. If we could find who did it, they could prove it in a minute."

Salter closed the file and pushed it away from him. "How long is it going to take me to read this stuff?" he asked.

"Three days. Maybe longer."

"I think I'll have a chat with this old friend first." Anything to postpone the labor of tackling those seven files.

"Why? He hadn't seen her lately."

"I know, but I'd like to get some idea of what she was like. What kind of ad did she put in the paper?"

Wycke read out the ad. "Attractive lady, late thirties, interested in sports—tennis, skiing—likes bridge, theater, reading, wishes to meet man with similar tastes with view to friendship."

"What kind of woman puts ads in the paper?"

"Hard to say. Would you?"

"Would I what?"

"Would you put an ad in the paper? 'Handsome, intelligent, sense of humor, late forties, all my own teeth, wishes to meet—' What would you like to meet?"

"Beautiful widow, large income, no hobbies."

"Seriously. It's a big step, isn't it?"

"It would be for me. I wonder if a woman would feel the same way?"

"Why don't you start with this Agnes Loomis woman? She was a pal of Cowell's."

"Right. Then she'll tell Gerry that I'm working like

a beaver." Salter leafed through the file again. "Where does she work?"

"She was working for the city temporarily when we talked to her in October. Organizing some kind of old folks' activities. She seemed to be into a lot of things."

"I'll find out from Gerry. She started this whole thing up again—Loomis, I mean." Salter closed the file and looked at Wycke. "You eating somewhere special today?"

Wycke looked at his watch. "You choose," he said.

This time they went to the small bar at the entrance to Sir John's, the restaurant in the basement of the Eaton Centre, not far from City Hall, a bar that Salter claimed served the best fish and chips in Toronto. On the way over, Wycke asked, "Started your Christmas shopping yet?"

"Finished," Salter said smugly. "All except for one thing. We've got a little silver birch tree in front of our house. Annie planted it five years ago, and she wants to decorate it with those white Christmas lights you see around Yorkville outside the classy boutiques. I've been keeping my eyes open, so has she, but no one seems to sell them. You think those places import them from the States?"

"Probably. Like those boots my wife bought last year. They're made in Montreal, but if you want to buy a pair you have to drive down to Freeport in Maine. They don't sell them here."

They reached the Eaton Centre and made their way past the lottery booth down to the bar. "If you see any little white lights around—outdoor ones—buy them for me, will you?" Salter asked.

While they were eating their fish and chips, Wycke said, "You a gourmet, Charlie? You follow those restaurant columns in the papers?"

"Follow them? I can't even understand them. Anyway, the last one I read recommended some place because it had 'crispy' tablecloths."

"You wouldn't want 'soggy' tablecloths, would you?" Wycke said, grinning.

Salter made a point of finding Gerry in her office at City Hall when there were enough people around so that he could avoid giving her a progress report ("I'll fill you in in a few days," he said) and got the information that Agnes Loomis was no longer working for the city, but was now being paid by the Ontario government to set up child-care communes. "That's how I ran into her again," Gerry said. "She wanted to get into the community centers to find the women who had problems getting their children looked after." She gave him Loomis's home phone number. Salter called, and finding her at home, made an arrangement to meet her there within the hour.

The house was on Montrose Street, south of Bloor, an unimproved three-story building on a street that had been well kept without too many signs of gentrification. Italian and Portuguese, Salter guessed, as he noticed the odd dead tomato plant in the front yards, the clean and occasionally gaudy paintwork—green fences picked out with red corner posts—and evidence that many of the women were at home. In the front yard of the house next to the one he sought there was a small shrine to the Madonna, lit by a ring of colored lights. Salter looked around and saw that many of the houses were sprouting their Christmas decorations around the porches and the windows; he made a firm mental note to dig his own out of the basement.

The woman who answered the door was dressed in a man's shirt, blue jeans, and thick work socks. Salter's first impression was that she was put together from the halves of two different women. From the waist up she was bony and flat-chested, with black, slightly tangled hair and a small round face with a nose like a tiny pyramid on which rested a pair of steel-rimmed glasses. Below the waist she was suddenly fat, so that the blue jeans looked painful where they stretched across her thighs.

"I think I can guess what you want, Inspector. You came to the right place. Come in," she said.

He stepped inside the house into the hall, past a room quite empty of furniture, where he saw that one wall had been half repainted and the paint roller lay drying in its tray.

She urged him forward. "One day I'll get this place finished," she said. "But I'll have to take the phone off the hook." She laughed, shaking her head. "We'll have to go to the kitchen."

There, seated at an old table that took up most of the room, a small round woman was drinking out of a mug, nodding and smiling at Salter as he came in. "Tea," Agnes Loomis said. "Tea. Let's all have some more tea," and pushed Salter toward a chair. She took the teapot off the table, swirled it around and poured him a large mug of the weakest tea he had ever been seriously offered. When he put milk into it, the result looked like the disinfectant he remembered as a child that was used to wash out the lavatories at the beaches.

"Have a cookie," she offered, proferring him a plate of flat gray biscuits. "These are made with canned milk and corn flour with caraway seeds, an old pioneer recipe. Don't sit there in your coat," she added loudly. "Make yourself at home." She looked across at the little fat lady. "He's waiting for us to tell him to take it off," she laughed.

Salter stood up and took off his raincoat and looked for somewhere to hang it.

"Anywhere," Mrs. Loomis said, waving her hand.

In the end he draped it over one of the kitchen chairs while she watched him approvingly. "You'll get used to us, won't he, Rose?" she said. "We don't have any rules here. How's the cookie?"

Salter bit into it and it crumbled all over his hand, filling his mouth with plaster dust. He wiped off the rubble around his lips and took out his notebook, clearing a work space among the crumbs on the table. "I'd like to ask you about Nancy Cowell," he began, glancing pointedly at Rose to make her go away. She nodded at him and drew her chair closer to the table. A youth appeared, about fifteen. "What's for supper, Mom?" he asked. "I've got basketball."

"Who knows?" Agnes Loomis said grandly. "Hot dogs, probably, unless you want to cook something else."

"We had hot dogs last night," the boy said. "It's your turn to cook tonight."

"I said I would cook supper if I had time, but I haven't had time, so hard cheese, old boy. Hot dogs it is." This was said with a flourish, as if for Salter's benefit, a feeling he confirmed when Rose hugged herself, grinning at the way Mrs. Loomis disposed of her family problems.

The boy went to a cupboard and found some cornflakes, which he poured into a bowl. He opened the refrigerator door. "There's no milk, Mom," he said.

"There's some here," his mother said, waving the carton. "If you want it all you'll have to get some more at Becker's before you go."

The boy poured some milk on his cornflakes and left the room, eating.

A door opened on the second floor; feet descended the stairs. "That you, Terry?" Mrs. Loomis called. "How did it go this afternoon? I didn't know you were home already."

"Fine," a voice called from halfway down the stairs.

"Come in and join us," her mother shouted through the door. "We've got a visitor."

And bring your friends, thought Salter, while he waited to begin.

A pretty blond girl of about fourteen came in and looked around the table.

"This is Inspector Salter," Loomis said. "From Metro's finest."

She turned to Salter. "Terry is on the swim team at school. They had a meet today against North Toronto. Are you hungry, honey? There's a new jar of peanut butter."

"No. I'll get something later." She looked at Salter and Rose and excused herself, going back up the stairs.

"I've got a family of athletes," Mrs. Loomis announced. "Now, what's your problem, Inspector?"

"I'd better go, Agnes," Rose said suddenly. "Fred will be in soon. I'll see you tomorrow."

"Bring him over for a cup of tea!"

"No, no, dear. He likes his dinner when he gets in."

Salter imagined Fred as weighing two hundred and fifty pounds, a road-builder, being invited to share the disinfectant tea and plaster cookies.

"You've got a ring through your nose," Agnes Loomis said, looking slightly at a loss at the way she was being deserted.

Finally they began. She cleared the decks by walking around the kitchen and closing off the cupboard doors that the boy had left open, just like someone getting ready to organize the kitchen for dinner.

"You think you're going to find the guy who killed Nancy?" she said, before Salter could ask his first question. She ran some water into the sink and began clearing the table.

"Did you know her well?"

"As well as anybody. I think I could have helped her."

"Was she broke, or sick?"

"She needed help," Loomis asserted. "But she wasn't broke or sick, no."

"Where did you meet her?"

"City Hall. I got talking to her. She seemed kinda lost."

"How was she lost?"

"Lonely, mostly. This dating thing she was into, for instance. Dating men she'd never met. I've got dozens of friends I was going to introduce her to. Some of them may seem kind of kooky until you get to know them, but they don't go around raping and killing people. She would have been safe with them." It was a defining remark that drew a line between her world and Salter's, the world of killers, rapists, and cops.

Salter ignored it.

"Did you always go to the St. Lawrence Market with her?" he asked.

"No, I just offered to show her. I love the market."

"How well did you know her? Did you see each other all the time?"

"Oh, once we started talking, I got to know her pretty well . . .

"When? When did you start talking?"

"About three weeks before she was killed. We went out for a beer after work. I took her to The Pretzel Bell —you know it?"

Salter nodded. "How many times did you meet her apart from that first time?"

"Three or four times in the two weeks before she was killed. She wanted to get into some of the stuff I do."

"You talked to her a lot then? About herself?"

"That's right. It was pretty obvious she needed someone to talk to."

"Did she tell you anything about herself? Any dates she had? Anything about her husband?"

"She said she was having trouble meeting the right kind of men."

"Her husband?"

"She never said much, but I could take a pretty good guess." She ranged herself back in her chair and put a foot on the chair next to her. "We all married them, Inspector. I had one once."

"But not now," Salter said, thinking, it figures.

"I told him to go and get another servant." The telephone rang and she went out to the hall to answer it. Salter heard her arranging to be at a meeting that night: "With my warpaint on." She returned to her chair. "That's the Annex crowd," she said. "I'm helping them to get up a petition to stop the distribution of junk mail. I can't stay long, though. We're going down to Jarvis tonight for a POP demonstration. You'd better tell your pals to be out in force."

"POP?"

"Parents Opposed to Prostitution."

"What do you plan to do?"

"We have signs, and we'll take pictures of the johns

as they pick up the girls. And we'll talk to the girls, see if we can find any who don't want to be there. I have to go because I have all the signs in my car, and I'll be watching you guys, too, if there's any confrontation."

There was the sound of someone coming down the stairs. The girl called from the hallway. "I'm going out for a hamburger. If Dennis calls, tell him I'll be home tonight."

"Okay, honey. Will you look after Michael tonight?"

"I'll be here." The door slammed.

"Michael's my seven-year-old," Loomis said.

Salter closed his unused notebook and stood up. "Thanks," he said. "If I need you again I can find you here?"

"If you're lucky, old buddy," Loomis said. "But someone usually knows where I am. Keep trying if you don't get me the first time."

Salter left the house and considered his problem. He still needed someone who could tell him something about the dead woman, what she was like. He wanted to form some sort of impression of her—for example, whether she would be careful about the men she invited up to her apartment. Loomis, he judged, was useless in this regard because she would never accept the terms of his questions until she had debated them. He needed to try other avenues.

He drove back to the office, where Sergeant Gatenby was reading the files that had been sent over from Homicide.

"How's it going, boss? Any arrests imminent?" Gatenby asked.

"I don't think I'm going to arrest anyone, Frank. I don't mind much because if I do arrest someone, then Homicide is going to be very pissed off. What I'm really trying to do is prove to my ex-wife that we didn't just say, 'Serves her right for having round heels.' I want to convince her that in a case like this, no matter what you do, the killer may be someone nobody has ever heard of. You remember that woman who accidentally drowned in her bathtub, according to the inquest, and six months later some guy in Kingston Penitentiary confessed to killing her? Well, this time we know she was strangled, but God knows if we'll ever get near the guy who did it. I'm simply doing everything that Homicide did before, so I can say it's been done twice." And, he thought, put on a small demonstration that even when prostitutes get murdered, we still look for Jack the Ripper.

"What's the next move?"

"I'm going to talk to someone who knew this woman. Where do I find this guy Tranby?"

Gatenby opened the file. "He's got an office nearby; he's in real estate. Here." Gatenby switched the file around so that Salter could read off the telephone number. Salter called Tranby's office, and a woman answered with the information that Tranby spent his time up at Mitcham, a village about forty miles north of Toronto. "We're putting in a new development there," she added. Salter called the Mitcham site and found Tranby in his office. He arranged to drive up to see him the following morning. "How do I get there?" he asked.

"You know Stouffville?" Tranby asked. "We're a little bit east and north. Use the four-oh-four and come up to the Stouffville road. Then drive east until you see the sign for the turnoff to Mitcham. It's about three kilometers north of there. I'm on Church Street, at the old hardware store. You'll see my sign outside. Around nine-thirty, then?"

Salter hung up and started to leaf through the file.

"Your wife called," Gatenby said. "She wants to know if you've thought about the tree yet."

"No, I haven't. What's there to think about? I'll buy a Christmas tree. What's the problem?"

Salter was lying. He knew that the question meant, "Have you thought how to make sure early enough that there is a tree available yet, a good tree that will stand up straight, and do you remember that the stand broke last year, and that a new one will have to be bought, one big enough so that the tree will not fall over even if it is straight?" Salter believed that the sale of Christmas trees was a racket, and he tried every year to get one cheap, and for a stand he had persevered with a tripod bought from Woolworth's in the first year of their marriage, a stand so flimsy that he had to nail it to a sheet of plywood for stability, and then Annie had to cover the sheet of wood as quickly as possible with gifts so that the living room did not look like a hardware store. Each year he swore he would buy a stand that would hold up a telegraph pole, and each year he balked at the price, as he did at the rising price of Christmas trees.

On the way home he stopped at the Avenue Road Food Store, checked the trees for straightness, found two that were suitable, noted the prices, and postponed a decision until he had had a chance to check around. It was still quite warm.

Chapter

4

The village of Mitcham lies about fifteen kilometers beyond Markham, the town with the highest per-capita income in Canada. The inhabitants of Markham, or those who contribute most to its reputation as the center of the rural rich, make (or made) their money in downtown Toronto, and have chosen Markham as the place to spend it because until recently it was possible to buy farmland in the area relatively cheaply, land on which they custom-built houses big enough to contain three and a half bathrooms and an open fieldstone fireplace. Sometimes the farmland contained an old tractor barn, which the new owner could modernize into stables for his children's horses. Swimming pools are standard, and tennis courts becoming common. Beyond Markham the countryside is in transition as the quest for rural living pushes northward, but the village of Mitcham at the moment is beyond the limit of this new gold rush.

Salter drove down the main street, noting that except for the obligatory antiques store, the village had none of the sparkle of rural gentrification of Markham itself. There were a handful of stores, one gas station, and a coffee shop, but even these were separated by ordinary houses and a couple of vacant lots. Turning left along Church Street, Salter spotted Tranby's sign immediately, and pulled up outside the former hardware store. Tranby was waiting and ushered him into a room now bare of hardware but still with the original pine counter running the length of the store. In front, where the customers used to gather, a half-dozen director's chairs with canvas seats and backs were grouped around a makeshift trestle table. On the counter, a coffee machine was just disgorging a fresh brew into its lower chamber, and Tranby moved over to stand beside it. "Coffee, Inspector?" he asked, as the last drops filtered through. Receiving Salter's assent, he poured out two cups and sat down beside the policeman.

"So," he said. "Still trying to track down the guy who did for Nancy, eh?"

Salter nodded and sipped his coffee. Tranby was a surprise: the voice on the phone had been energetic and interested—the voice of someone in a sweater and with a big smile. The man sipping his coffee was dressed in a very lightweight gray tweed suit, an Irish-looking oatmeal-colored shirt with a dark green cloth tie, and paper-thin brown loafers. His hair lay tight to his head in neat, dark crinkles, graying evenly around the ears. Even now, when he spoke, his voice seemed incongruous, as if borrowed from someone else.

"Do you mind if I smoke?" Tranby asked.

Salter shook his head, surprised. "It's your office," he pointed out, and watched as Tranby opened an unfamiliar-looking packet of cigarettes, lit one, then replaced both cigarettes and lighter in different inside pockets of his jacket.

When he was settled, Salter said, "Tell me about Nancy Cowell. I'm trying to get some idea of what she was like."

"You want some background on Nancy and on Victor, right? I know Victor well—I was his best friend in college and we've stayed pretty close ever since, so I knew Nancy, too, though I can't say I was ever very close to her. She didn't have quite the same background as Vic, and I was a bit surprised when they got married."

"Tell me her story. What kind of person was she?"

"I'll start from when I first knew her, shall I?" Tranby arranged himself in his chair. "She was from River Heights; we both went to Kelvin High, though she was a few years behind me and I never really noticed her at school. River Heights, by the way, is the old English district. Her name was Catchpole before she married Vic."

"Rich family?"

"No, *old*. Even her grandfather was born in Winnipeg, I think. As a matter of fact, her grandfather and mine were in the grain business together."

Salter thought of something. "There's no mention of her family in the file. Why didn't they figure in the original inquiry?"

"Her father is dead, killed in the last war, and her mother is in a mental home. Nancy was an only child."

"And Kowalczyk? What's his background?"

"Ukrainian. North End Winnipeg. His father was a construction laborer and his mother got married straight from home. She doesn't know much outside the family. His brother really started the family climb—he's a lawyer in Calgary now—and I think he put Vic through engineering school."

"When did he change his name?"

"That was his brother. When he graduated from law school he persuaded the whole family to change their name to Cowell for business reasons." Tranby looked at Salter, and continued. "At that time you couldn't blame him. Things have changed a lot since then. I know Vic was getting uncomfortable with the new name, as his brother had been, I guess, by the old one, and when Nancy left him he changed back to Kowalczyk." Tranby smiled. "I still can't get used to it, because all the time I've known him he's been Vic Cowell. I think Nancy's leaving him had something to do with it."

"Why did she leave him?"

"You can ask Vic that."

"I will, but I'd like to hear your version."

"More coffee?" Tranby asked.

Salter declined, and Tranby began again. "All right. But remember this is just my impression. Not to be used. Okay?"

Salter nodded.

"I think Vic just couldn't stand her anymore."

"Why?"

"He thought she was two-timing him."

"Was she?"

Tranby rearranged himself in his chair, crossing his legs and laying his tie flat on his chest. "He caught her once," he said. "Not that once is so bad. What are the statistics—fifty percent?" Tranby shrugged it off. "But Vic couldn't stand the idea. He's from a different culture and he still hangs on to it."

"But she was screwing around after they were married, right?"

"Just once that I know of, but Vic thought there was more. You see, Inspector, I don't know what she was doing, I just know what Vic thought, and he thought she was. You have to understand, for him she was the golden girl, the prize, the queen of the ball, literally from another world. His mother didn't think so—his father was killed, by the way, when a tunnel collapsed while he was digging it—she was against Nancy from the start. You know anything about the Ukrainian culture?" Once again Tranby glanced at Salter confidentially.

"Not much; tell me," Salter said.

"Okay." Tranby nodded. "We're talking about twenty years ago, remember," he said. "Even then Vic's mother would have been old-fashioned, so let's go back forty years. Okay?"

"If you say so," Salter said.

"Well, back then, traditional Anglo families in Winnipeg did not look favorably on Ukrainian sons-in-law. If the daughter fell in love with a Ukrainian boy, and there was enough money about, she got sent on a trip to visit relatives in England. The same thing happened if a girl got pregnant. And vice versa. Ukrainian mothers watched their daughters very carefully, and when an Anglo boy showed up on the doorstep, the girl would find herself staying for the summer on her uncle's farm near Edmonton. This was Winnipeg, remember, a long time ago, but there's still a bit of it left."

Salter speculated on the possibility of a family feud, settled in blood. "Did the marriage cause problems?" he asked.

"With Vic's mother, sure, and with all the uncles and aunts and all the old babushka generation. But Vic's brother thought Nancy was great, and he persuaded the old lady to accept it."

So much for family revenge.

"They met in college, you say."

"That's right. She was the engineering queen the year Vic and I graduated. Vic was in charge of the prom, and that year the medics tried to kidnap the queen, as usual, but Vic had the job of guarding her and he substituted another girl and arranged to have *her* kidnapped by the aggies."

"The who?"

"The agricultural students. It's too complicated to go into, but he fooled the medics and the Winnipeg media—he was feeding them with the story of the fake kidnapping. Vic pretended to blame the medics, who knew they didn't have her; then he arranged a little leak that it was the aggies who had her, who'd got the jump on the medics. Then the medics found out where the aggies had this girl and they turned up at the farm, pretending to be engineers who had been warned that the medics would try something like this. It worked, and the medics kidnapped the wrong girl and by the time they realized it, Nancy was being crowned queen. She had spent the previous two days in Minneapolis, escorted by Vic. With another couple of engineers as chaperones."

"You should have made a movie of it," Salter said. "With Ronald Reagan."

"Didn't they do this kind of stuff in Toronto, then?"

"I wouldn't know." Salter had dropped out of college in his second year, but he didn't mind if Tranby thought it was the eighth grade. "So this was when it all happened?" he asked.

"Yes. Vic started taking her out then, and they got married after she graduated."

"And then he started getting jealous?"

"Not right away. But this was in the swinging sixties, remember, and even Winnipeg started to swing. Rumors started to fly about what everybody was doing —everybody else, of course." Tranby smiled. "The parties got kind of lively, and you started to hear about wife swapping. Remember?"

"I wasn't there," Salter said.

"Yeah, but . . ." Tranby looked quizzical. "Well, anyway, let me put it like this. Nancy wanted to go to all of the parties and Vic didn't, and sometimes she went without him."

"On her own?"

"Yeah, I think she was just asserting her independence. And maybe she was curious. But Vic's mother heard some of it and she nagged Vic and it caused problems."

"Was she screwing around?"

"I don't know that she was screwing *around,*" Tranby said. "But like I told you, she got caught once coming out of a motel on the Pembina Highway at three o'clock in the afternoon."

"Who caught her?"

"Vic. Then he kicked her out, or tried to, because she left before he could."

Salter considered the scenario. "You were his pal," he said. "What did you think of it all?"

When Tranby spoke, his voice had a measured judicial tone. "I think we have to understand the difference between Vic and Nancy, Inspector. Vic grew up in a world of nice girls and sluts, and he stayed that way. But over in River Heights, the times were changing; maybe they always were different. The odd affair would be no big deal to someone like Nancy, as I tried to tell

Vic, but it was to him. He wanted Sleeping Beauty, and that's what he thought he was getting, so if Nancy did have a little romance after they were married, it would have been a very big thing to someone like Vic."

And to me, buddy, thought Salter. "So Nancy Cowell was liberated, was she? And he wasn't? That it?"

"That'll do, I guess. She was a real sweetheart, and he's a prince of a guy, but it was East and West."

"Did you see much of her, here in Toronto, I mean?"

"I got in touch with her a couple of times. I think she was hoping to get back with Vic, and I'm still his best friend, I guess, and I would have done anything for them. So we met a couple of times, but not for a while now. She could have called me anytime, but she never did. That's about it. I never really tried to persuade her to go back to him, or anything like that."

"Why? The way you talk you were pretty sympathetic to both of them."

"It would never have worked out. Vic's not going to change now, and he would always be suspicious of where she spent her afternoons."

"Was he a violent man?" A loaded question. Salter moved to explain himself. "Did he ever lay hands on his wife, after he saw her leaving this motel, for instance?"

Tranby got up to get himself more coffee. "I don't know about that," he said. "Maybe. He lit out after the guy she was with, I know. Some people at the motel had to separate them."

"Who was the guy? Do you know?"

"Some book salesman from Toronto, Vic said. I just heard the story of the fight from a friend of Nancy's, I think."

Salter said, "According to you she left because she couldn't stand his jealousy anymore. But did she tell you he ever hurt her?"

"She didn't say. She just said she'd had enough."

Salter waited to see if Tranby would continue. The other man sipped his coffee for a few moments, then lit a cigarette, slightly turned away from Salter, to show he was thinking. Then he said, "Have you ever read a book called *The Great Gatsby*?"

Who the hell hasn't, thought Salter. Once in high school and once all by myself.

"I think so," he said. "Didn't they make a movie out of it?"

"Two. The first one was better, but neither one really got to the heart of the book."

Salter said nothing, wondering why he was being treated to a discourse on the movies.

Tranby continued. "I think Vic was a kind of Gatsby and Nancy was his Daisy, except that Vic got his Daisy and then realized she wasn't the girl he had dreamed about."

"Didn't Gatsby get killed?" Salter asked. "He did in the movie."

"Sure, but you see what I mean," Tranby pleaded.

"This time, though, it's Daisy who gets killed, a different ending, like," Salter said, assuming a yokel pose. He was thinking to himself that Tranby's fancy analogy made him less rather than more reliable as a character witness, because, having written his own script, he would be more concerned to show its validity than think anymore about what Kowalczyk or Cowell were really like. An armchair sociologist.

"Yes, but the idea is the same, don't you see? Nancy the golden girl and Vic Cowell the self-made man."

"That's how you saw them, is it? Did you ever warn your pal how the story comes out?"

Tranby looked at a loss. "What?" he asked. "Oh, no. This is just an idea I had to try and explain to you how Vic saw Nancy. Oh, no. I thought about all this after Nancy got killed."

"Okay, thanks. As far as you know, did she have any or many boyfriends in Toronto?"

"I don't know. She didn't say."

Salter put his coffee cup on the table and stood up. "Your pal, Kowalczyk," he asked. "Is he doing well?"

"He's a millionaire. One of the biggest developers in the West. He's got projects in all the major cities. He's the one who's backing me here." Tranby pointed to an architectural model on the counter. "Want to see it?" he asked.

He walked over to the model: a small street lined with old-fashioned stores; behind the stores on one side was a huge parking lot. Salter looked more closely and saw that most of the stores were specialty food stores—delicatessens, French bakeries, and high-class butchers and fishmongers.

"We're calling it the Mitcham Marketplace," Tranby said. "See here." He pointed to an area of the street that was covered but not enclosed. "We are going to rent space to selected market gardeners in the area so that we have really fresh produce. We've tried to reproduce the atmosphere of a turn-of-the-century small town."

"Here?" Salter said, realizing suddenly where he was. "In this place?"

"Right." Tranby looked triumphant. "The street is the one you are on now." He pointed out the window.

"You're going to tear down this street and build this?" Salter asked.

Tranby nodded. "First-class shopping in a real market atmosphere," he said. "The street will be cobbled, and we've created some new designs for gas lamps."

"Who will shop here?" Salter asked.

"This is a catchment area for a big pool of discriminating consumers," Tranby said. "They can drive a couple of miles and spend a morning or an afternoon here, knowing that every store is worth visiting. We've invited a couple of good restaurants in Toronto to participate. It's a new concept. People with money and leisure have rediscovered shopping as a leisure activity, but they like to feel special when they're buying their groceries. We're creating a special market for special people."

"Did you dream this up?" Salter now heard Tranby's voice clearly; it was the voice of a man on a high, excited by a vision.

"We've been working on it for about a year. We've got options on just about all the real estate we need, and now the stores are starting to come in."

"And Kowalczyk is in this?" Salter asked, wondering if this was how millions got made.

"He's backing me personally. I showed him the concept a few months ago when he was in Toronto, and he offered to lend me the money. It's a partnership that's developing the site, and I have to put up my share of the seed money for designs and stuff like that." Tranby looked at his model, touching the roof of one of the houses with a soft finger. "When we've finished, I'll give Vic back his money."

Behind the model, pinned to the wall, was a blown-up photograph of the original street, the "before" of the model's "after." There was nothing special about it, but the idea of wiping out a turn-of-the-century street to build a toytown version of what it should have looked like irritated some conservative dog-in-the-manger corner of Salter's being. "Good luck," he said neutrally.

"It's going to revitalize the area," Tranby said. "Give it a focus."

"I guess it will," Salter said. "You saw Kowalczyk that weekend, didn't you? How did he seem?"

Tranby nodded. "We had lunch and settled the loan before he went off to his cottage. I stayed around to tidy up some stuff, and I was still in Winnipeg when the news came through on Sunday, so I stayed a couple of days to be with him."

"Did he talk about his wife much?"

"That's mostly what we talked about. He'd had a letter from her recently."

"Did he? What about?"

"She wanted to give it another try."

"And how did he react to that?" There was no mention of this in the file.

Tranby considered the question carefully. "Hopeful, I think. Very hopeful that there was some way he could forget all the bad times she had given him and they could get back together."

"Do you know what she said in her letter?"

"Yes, he showed it to me."

"What did you think? Did you think they had a chance?"

"When you think of the whole history you'd have to call it just a chance, wouldn't you?"

"You mean the affair in Winnipeg?"

"And the way he reacted to it."

"Did you offer him any advice? About his wife?"

Tranby looked at Salter for a long time, then pulled his head into his shoulders and fixed his gaze on the table. "I had a problem, didn't I? This guy was my oldest friend. He'd had some rotten times with this marriage, and here he was thinking of going into it again. Of course, most of it was his own fault. I liked Nancy and she was no different from her age, I guess, but Vic is a very old-fashioned guy. I didn't want him to get his hopes up. I wanted him to be a bit realistic about what he might find in Toronto."

"What did you tell him?"

"I told him to take her for what she was."

"What did you say, exactly?"

"I can't remember. I think I warned him that she might have had a boyfriend or two."

"And what was his reaction?"

"I don't think he shrugged it off."

"So, when you left him, did he plan to come to town or not?"

"I thought he planned to come, yes."

"When?"

"The following weekend. But I never was alone with him to talk about it after that. I haven't had a chance to get back to Winnipeg since then."

Salter pondered this act of friendship. He could understand Tranby's reasons—he might have done the same thing himself. It took some courage, too. But if Tranby had not tried to prepare his friend, was it possible that Nancy Cowell might still be alive?

Tranby said, "I guess, in a way, people like Nancy are the victims of the sexual revolution, aren't they? One more thing we can blame on the pill."

"You don't think much of the new freedom?"

"No, no. I'm just quoting what the Mrs. Grundys say. As a matter of fact, when I got divorced I got a vasectomy so I wouldn't get caught again." Tranby changed the topic. "Do you mind if I say that I hope you don't catch the guy? Vic is pretty well used to the idea that his wife was killed by some weirdo. If you catch the guy and it's someone she's been dating or something, there'll be the whole courtroom hearing of what kind of life she was leading and all that stuff. Vic thinks it was an accident, one of those things that can happen in Toronto. It would hit him hard if it was proved that she was sleeping with every guy she met. I hope sleeping dogs lie." He smiled a little at the unintentional play on words. "I'm sorry now that I said anything to him myself."

"We don't know that she was, do we? The boys in Homicide tell me that the chances are very good that she was just a chance victim, that it could have been anybody. They also tell me that we won't catch him anyway, so you're probably going to get your wish." He stood up. "Who else knew that Kowalczyk was planning to come to Toronto? You have any idea?"

"How do you mean?" Tranby asked, looking slightly startled. "His mother, I guess. And his sister."

"You didn't meet anyone on Friday afternoon and tell them?"

"No. I was busy all afternoon, and after dinner I just stayed in my room and watched television. The weather was lousy."

Salter stood up and walked to the door. Tranby followed him.

"Doesn't look like much, does it?" Tranby said as the two men looked out on Church Street. "But wait until next year."

Salter said nothing, apparently sharing Tranby's vision. Then, "This cottage of his. Did he use it much?"

"Whenever he could get away. He liked to fish, and

he enjoyed doing things to it. I helped him fix it up. We're both really engineers still, you know. We like to play with construction. How about you, Inspector? You like to tinker?"

"Only when there's someone who knows what he's doing to help me," Salter said. "Was Kowalczyk's cottage hard to get to?"

"Not in the summer. There's a road that goes right by his place. But it's pretty isolated once you're in there."

Salter pointed to the street. "You've got a customer," he said as a pink Cadillac rolled toward them and stopped. "I've got to get back to work. Good luck with the marketplace. You'll be here if I need anymore help?"

"Night and day, Inspector, until we turn the streetlights on," Tranby said.

Salter left and drove back to Toronto, this time taking the Markham road so that he could have a good look at Canada's richest neighborhood. Driving along Markham's main street, he got some idea of what Tranby was dreaming about. Although he had passed by in sightless fashion often enough, he was surprised when he looked at how much refurbishing the main street had undergone under the influence of the local prosperity. But where do the poor shop? he wondered, and got his answer when he turned right on Highway 7 and passed a huge mall with the familiar mix of chain retail outlets and fast-food concessions. Then he wondered if Tranby was in the right business, remembering a famous merchandising tag he had read somewhere: "Don't soak the rich, soak the poor. There's more of them."

Back in the office, Salter reluctantly picked up the copies of the letters from the men who had answered Nancy Cowell's advertisement. Reluctantly, because he had already looked them over and they told a sad story, to him, a story of dozens, thousands, of people in Toronto who wanted someone to talk to, and eat dinner with, and perhaps rape.

He had not been aware that perfectly normal, sensible women would put an advertisement in a newspaper asking to meet men, and had talked about it to Annie, who asked around the advertising agency where she worked and came back with the information that, although everybody wasn't doing it, far more were than even she had imagined.

"They don't want to go to singles bars. And the gatherings you hear about generally gather seven women to every man, so they advertise," she told him.

"How does it work?"

"Leslie told me—she's done it. You put an ad in and tell them to write to a box number. Then you sort out the replies and write back to the reasonable ones, agreeing to meet. Then the man writes back arranging a time and place, right out in the open, generally a restaurant, and you go dutch. Then you take it from there."

"What are they looking for, people like Leslie?"

"They want to meet people."

"Not sex?"

"Leslie says some women are. But not Leslie, or not only, I guess. She wants to meet some new men. For company."

"But she wants to meet *men.*"

"Oh, sure. Sex is one of the things they have in mind, but not unless it works out that way, as it might if she met a man in the old way. The point is that she's hoping to meet men, and if she could meet them normally, she would. After the first meeting it's just like any other relationship."

"But does she ever have any luck? I can't imagine any of the guys *I* know putting an ad in the paper, or answering one."

"Why?"

Salter thought about it carefully, and as far as he could, honestly. "Because they would feel like losers if they did. And they would assume the women would all be dogs."

"You've met Leslie. Is she a dog? I would call her normal even by police standards."

"Don't get up tight. I'm trying to tell you the way it is."

"Well, for God's sake, maybe your pals should try it. As you say, the reason why none of your pals would advertise, why *you* wouldn't, is because they live in a total muddle of macho pride, and you wouldn't admit to yourself that you're lonely because you think that's something to be ashamed of. Maybe women are more realistic, tougher, not so screwed up. They can admit they have a problem—they're lonely, and it's not their fault, so they can do something about it. Why do you think these women outnumber the men seven to one at these rendezvous get-togethers—*seven to one,* Leslie said. Because there are seven times as many losers among women? That's crap. It's because they're doing something about it; they don't care if somebody they know sees them there. But the reason those things don't work, apart from the odds, Leslie says, is that the only guys who go really *are* losers. When a normal man like you gets lonely, first he thinks it's temporary, then he looks in the mirror and waits for something to turn up. If something does turn up it's because some woman, seeing the signs, takes the initiative and picks him up. Most men won't make a move until they've got all the signs saying they won't be rejected. Women think differently. They've grown up being looked over by you guys and being rejected. They're used to it. So they look in the mirror and think they're all right, and they put an ad in the paper. Little do they know that all the *normal* guys are sitting in their little lonely apartments, watching television and hoping to bump into the woman of their dreams while they're putting out the garbage."

"Jesus, Annie, calm down."

"I feel sorry for Leslie. She puts an ad in the paper so you think there must be something wrong with her because if any of Metro's finest did it there would be something wrong with *him*. And there probably would be, but Leslie has to take that chance. Just think of all the creeps she has to sift through, hoping for once that someone half-decent has gotten his nerve up, or swallowed his pride."

"Take it easy. I'm just trying to find out what goes on these days."

"Anyway, maybe you're wrong." Annie was now in full flight, moving around the kitchen, banging down pots, wiping already-clean counters, generally buttoning up the kitchen as if she were preparing to leave. "Maybe things have changed a bit since you and I met. It is possible that there are some men, a few anyway, who think like women now, who've left behind some of the male bullshit. So maybe Leslie will meet a forty-seven-year-old policeman whose wife has left him, who is looking to meet a nice lady. Leslie says she's had a bit of luck with European men, who don't think twice about announcing that they would like to meet someone like her. In Europe, she says, it's normal to advertise, so maybe what we're talking about is some phony American image you guys have of yourselves."

Salter had a number of ways to go. If he tried to meet the argument, it would go on until one of them said something that the other would not want to hear, and the trouble with letting it all hang out, in Salter's experience, was the difficulty of stuffing it all back in. Or he could cut the argument off, but in Annie's present mood that might be interpreted as male bullying. He took a third route, appearing to consider her speech thoughtfully, trying to learn something from it, a tactic he had used in the past. "All the guys I know *are* North American," he said mildly.

"Don't I know it," Annie said, a totally meaningless remark.

"European or not," he continued, "I think a lot of guys who answer ads like this aren't looking for companionship. Maybe European women know this and come armed, but from what you say, women like Leslie don't realize what they might be getting themselves into. In North America, I mean."

"Oh, they realize it. They know men and women are different. They know that women don't often commit rape or abuse children sexually or any other of the things that keep you guys busy. But that difference may not be biological, you know. Maybe men are conditioned to need assault as part of sex. Women aren't. I'm not, anyway."

I've been here before, Salter thought, as he listened to his wife echo Gerry's theme.

"Where did you read this?" he asked.

"What's that supposed to mean?"

"You're talking about some theory of the way men and women are that I haven't heard from you before. Where did you read it?"

"I didn't. But I work with women who do read and I've been listening to them."

"Okay. But right now could we talk about the way

things are, not *why* they are that way? I don't feel qualified."

"Maybe you should do something about it." The words were still aggressive but Annie had subsided now, literally onto the couch (still holding a dish towel) and emotionally as well, most of her passion spent.

"I'm trying to. But give me a hand, will you? Tell me what you think of these letters."

"I've got to put the laundry in first. And you can give *me* a hand."

Salter dutifully stood in the way while Annie filled the washer and dryer, and ten minutes later they came back upstairs. He skimmed through the letters and separated them into three piles. Then he poured himself a beer and helped Annie to the dregs of a bottle of wine and started in.

"First of all, I'm right, and so are you," he said. He handed her a group of six letters. The first three had much in common; they described themselves as happily married men who were often in Toronto and were looking for a little diversion on the side.

"They're honest, anyway," Annie said when she had read them. "Stupid, too, though. They think only frustrated women advertise."

"Right. It's not true, as you say, but these guys think it is, and if Leslie met them and turned them down, they might get a little rough."

Annie brushed this off. "No problem. No woman in her right mind would bother with creeps like that even if she was just interested in sex. Look at this one; he says three times he's a bit strapped for money just to let her know that his services are available but she might have to pay for his dinner."

The next letter sent her eyebrows up. It was from a man aged twenty-four who "specialized" in relationships with women between forty and seventy. He had just concluded a very satisfactory relationship with a woman of sixty-two.

"It's a form letter, too," Annie said. "He probably sends out hundreds." She put it aside.

The fifth letter was elaborately obscene: two closely typed, photocopied pages of what the author most enjoyed doing. Annie set this aside quickly and picked up the last one. It was like a breath of fresh air—cheerful, friendly, and inviting. "This looks all right," she said. "What's it doing in this pile?"

"Look at the one before. See the postscript?"

Annie stared at the handwritten note on the bottom of the photocopied fantasy, and then back at the last letter. "It's the same person," she said.

"Right," Salter said. "So you can't always tell, can you?"

"He wouldn't turn up," Annie said promptly. "He gets his jollies writing on bathroom walls. What about the rest?"

Next they sifted through twenty letters that told, collectively, a tale of lonely, sad men, staring out of windows, letters that showed that there were indeed men who were prepared to come out of the woodwork in response to an invitation; but on the whole they did not offer much hope for Leslie and her friends. Many of the letters were almost illiterate, or written in a species of acquired English that suggested there was a great deal of loneliness, more than the average, among middle-aged immigrants. They wrote often from rural addresses around Ontario, seeming to see in an advertisement in a Toronto paper the possibility of breaking out of the silence of a farmhouse where the woman has died. Nearly all of them described themselves as young for their years, and in possession of a steady income; they said they took a drink occasionally, but, usually, did not smoke. Collectively they were interested in books, dancing, raising dogs, and watching public-affairs shows on television. One of them offered at the first meeting to situate himself at a corner table of the restaurant of her choice so that she could look him over before she decided if she wanted to meet him.

The third pile consisted of five letters marked "Yes," and they looked back and found that all the others had a cross in the top right-hand corner.

"Two of these guys can prove they were out of town that weekend. Two others I'm going to have come into the office, but we don't really suspect them. The fifth one we can't find." He drew a sheet of paper from the bottom of the pile. "The first one met her for a drink in a pub in the Eaton Centre, one of those Duke places."

"What's that?"

"You know, those English pubs they send over here in a crate all ready to assemble complete with signs. He says that was the only time they met."

"Why?"

"He doesn't know. He says she wouldn't give him her phone number and she never called him back. He says she insisted on buying her own drink and that he liked her. He works as an editor for a press agency, and he's certainly okay because he was on duty that night at eleven."

"What about this one?"

"He says he met her once and didn't like her. He lives with his sister and says he was home in bed by twelve, which she confirms . . ."

"Why can't you find the last one?"

Salter told her.

"The two who were out of town—did they date her after the first meeting?"

"They say not."

"She didn't have much luck, did she?"

Salter considered. "Maybe five drinks with guys. No, I suppose not, but each one was probably more interesting than watching television, at least the looking forward to it. One of them might have been all right."

Annie nodded. "Leslie knows a girl who knows a girl who is marrying someone she met through an ad. What do you do next?"

"I'm going to talk to these two tomorrow. And I'm thinking of going to Winnipeg to talk to her husband."

They sat in silence for a while, watching a nature show that demonstrated that orangutans have not developed aggressive instincts.

"God, I feel lucky," Annie said when the program was over.

"Huh?"

"Lucky. Lucky I don't have to put ads in the paper, and if I say no, you won't beat me up."

"Good. Can I make a speech now?"

"What about?"

"A speech. Like yours."

"What do you mean?"

"I mean I want to say something without getting into an argument."

Annie said nothing, waiting.

"I'm Charlie Salter," he said. "Your husband. Not one of 'you guys.' We've been married for eighteen years and it's been good. Very good. Still is. But it won't be if we get into a lot of shouting about men and women. You aren't a 'woman' to me, someone to cook the meals, clean the house, and jump on when I feel like it. You're Annie. I spend a lot of time thinking about you, and I think I'm very lucky. When you're fed up about something I get very insecure wondering if it's my fault and what I can do about it. I don't think 'goddamn women.' I think, 'What's the matter with Annie?' As for my attitude to women generally, maybe you're right. I don't know. Just now I was trying to tell you the way most guys like me would react to being lonely. Maybe Seth and Angus will be different. I'm prepared to think about why things are this way. It's a rotten world for women and it's time it changed, eh? I'll see if I can help. But in the meantime, don't call me names. I'm not one of 'you guys.' I'm me. Let's start from there."

After a while, Annie said, "It was depressing and frightening hearing about what those girls have to put up with just to stop being lonely."

By a superhuman effort of will, Salter kept his mouth shut. He had made his speech, given it his best shot. Anything now would only dilute it. Beside him he thought he felt Annie organizing her emotions. The news from Buffalo came on the screen—a murder, two fires, and the arrest of a man with half a million dollars' worth of cocaine concealed in a bag of Kitty Litter in his basement. But no rapes. Salter stood up and switched it off. "Let's go to bed," he said.

Annie put the dirty glasses in the sink and went upstairs as Salter switched out the lights and followed her up. They undressed in silence and slid under the comforter, settling into their own sides of the bed, and lay still, waiting. It was not a night to lie staring at the ceiling, separated by the differences between men and women; nor was it a night for any of the fond horseplay Salter sometimes brought into the bedroom.

It was a night to be careful.

In the office, to Gatenby, he said, "Two of them can prove they were out of town; two others have pretty good stories, but I'll talk to them myself. The last one we haven't found, and we aren't likely to." He handed the letters to the sergeant, who read them through while Salter tidied his desk. It was Friday afternoon and nearly late enough to quit.

"You want me to try to find this one?" Gatenby asked.

"How? There's no address. Nothing to go on. What do you suggest? Advertise?"

"Sort of," Gatenby said. "Leave it to me."

Salter stared at his sergeant. "Good luck," he said. "You'll let me know your methods, will you?"

"I've just got an idea," Gatenby said, smiling to himself.

Salter brooded for about two seconds at this show of initiative, and then remembered again that it was Friday afternoon. "Got your Christmas shopping done yet, Frank?" he asked.

"Nearly. I've got something for the wife. We just have to buy a gift for my nephew now because we're spending Christmas with the wife's sister. My sister-in-law is easy; all she ever wants is another piece of china. She must have a basement full of the stuff. Still, buy them what they want, eh? I've been hinting for twenty years that I'd like one of those Swiss army knives like you got for Angus, only I'd like the one with everything on it, including a shaving mirror."

"Why the hell don't you buy yourself one?"

"It wouldn't be the same. Besides, it's getting to be a game. Every year I walk Martha round the knife shops, pointing them out, saying how terrific they are, but she never catches on. And if I did buy myself one . . ."

". . . that would be the year she bought me/you one for Christmas," the two men said together.

"Right," said Gatenby. "See my problem?"

"What are you getting Martha?" Salter asked, trying to guess from images of slippers and vacuum cleaners and electric kitchen implements.

"A pair of tickets to the Blue Jays' home games," Gatenby said.

"Baseball tickets?" Salter stared at him.

"She's got everything else, and she's mad about baseball. I hate the bloody game, so this way I'm saying that I don't mind if she goes without me."

"Who will she go with?"

"Her nephew probably. Who cares?"

"Aren't you afraid she'll run off with the pitcher one day?"

"I'm more afraid she'll buy another television set and lock herself in the spare room when there's a home game on."

"What about the nephew? How old is he?"

"Twelve. He's easy, too. He read this book about a kid who got to Wimbledon and played John McEnroe, and he wants a tennis racket."

"You've got it all wrapped up, haven't you? Let's pack up, Frank. I'm meeting Annie on the Roof to start our Christmas shopping."

Salter made bustling motions and the sergeant left. When the door was closed, he took out his list and added "Gatenby—one Swiss army knife" and ticked it off, all in one entry. Annie can give it to him, he thought. We'll have them over for a drink. It was her idea.

"You think Seth would like a tennis racket?" he said to Annie as they sipped their first drink. She was already loaded with parcels from the afternoon's shopping, and they were discussing the remaining names on the list.

"A what?"

"A tennis racket. It was just an idea."

"He's never said a word about wanting to play tennis. He wants books. He's given me a list."

"Did you get him any?"

"I got three. That's enough."

"Good. That's done then."

"And *you* can buy Angus a sheepskin jacket. Mother wants to give him one and she's asked me to do it for her."

"Where?"

"Find out."

"What size is he?"

"Find out."

"How much should I pay?"

"Make up your own mind."

"That's settled then. What else do we have to get tonight?" He recognized that the sheepskin jacket was one of those tasks, like the ones in fairy tales, that husbands have to do without asking questions, tasks they are given whenever the wife feels tired of carrying the whole load, which was not very often, thank God.

Annie produced her list and handed it over. It ran to about thirty items, including a new angel for the top of the tree and a gift for Annie's godmother, a rich old lady whom Salter had never seen, who lived in Florida, and who sent Annie five dollars on her birthday every year.

Salter looked the list over. "Let's get going," he said. "We only have three weeks." Then he smiled brightly to disprove any suggestion of sarcasm.

On Saturday Annie had an idea. They had spent the whole day doggedly working their way down the list and Salter had his feet up in front of the television waiting for the round, smiling face to stop talking and let the film he was chatting about begin. Annie, who was making a fresh list from the wreckage of the old one, suddenly said, "Tree."

"I'll get it," Salter said firmly, fearing a discussion that would interfere with the first few minutes of *Great Expectations*, his favorite movie sequence.

But Annie had an idea, a real "why-don't-you." "Why don't you take Seth and cut your own tree?" she suggested.

"Cut my own?" Salter asked, keeping his eyes on Magwich. "What are you talking about?"

"The paper is full of ads for tree farms where you can cut your own tree. Seth would enjoy that."

Salter considered while Pip was being caned by his sister. His instincts howled to him that it was a bad, ill-thought-out idea, and he tried to formulate the messages that were informing them. "I don't have an ax," he said, "or a chain saw, or one of those two-handled jobs."

"They'll supply the tools," she said. "It'll be fun."

"Then why don't you come too?"

"I've got to do something about the rest of this list, and make the shortbread."

Salter considered the problem thoughtfully. He didn't want this discussion going on after they caught Magwich. "All right," he said. "Pick out a tree farm and write the address down for me. And tell Seth." Joe Gargery had just delivered his shining line, graciously forgiving Magwich for stealing his pie. The next good scene was the fight with Herbert Pockett, which gave him time to get a beer from the refrigerator.

The next morning the weather seemed to be continuing in its mild autumn mode as Salter and his younger son prepared to depart. The knowledge that he was once more embarking on an enterprise that he didn't know anything about but ought to, like killing and cleaning a chicken, made him irritable. Seth appeared dressed in parka, mitts, boots, and woolly hat. Salter looked at Annie. "It's fifty above, for God's sake. He'll roast in that lot," he said.

"Then he can take something off. The tree farm is forty miles away. It might be cold there."

Salter put on his raincoat and rubbers and found a pair of old gloves to handle the sharp pine needles. "Let's go, son," he said, and they headed north.

The snow began about thirty miles past the 401 highway. By the time Salter found the tree farm there was an inch of it on the ground, and the temperature had dropped to below freezing. A dozen cars were parked in the yard of the farm, and Salter pulled in and looked around for some activity. A sign pointed them toward an assembly point. They walked down a narrow pathway through the trees to where a group of men were waiting beside a flatbed farm trailer that was hitched up to, possibly, the last farm horse in Ontario. As Salter got closer he began to wish he had listened to the forecast and made some inquiries about how you go about cutting down your own tree. All the men were dressed in quilted garments; several of them had hats with little earflaps, and most were heavily booted, one in a pair of three-climbers that laced up to his knees. Salter put on his gloves and buttoned his raincoat to the neck.

"You coming with us?" the tree farmer asked him. "You got anything to cut your tree with?"

Salter shook his head. When he looked around he saw that every man had an ax, or a saw. The man with the lace-up boots had both, as well as a hooked implement, a device for grappling logs from fast-flowing rivers.

The owner started to shake his head while the other men shook their heads at each other in pairs. The man with the lace-up boots stepped forward. "You can use mine," he said. "Here, I'll give you a hand onto the trailer." He put a hand under Salter's elbow. Seth moved to the front of the trailer to watch the owner handle the reins.

In the woods the snow was already four or five inches deep; after a journey of about four hundred yards, the trailer stopped, and the owner indicated where they could cut. Salter tucked his pants into his socks and followed his new friend to the tree of his choice. He watched the man take it down neatly with his saw and then trim it with his ax. When the man was satisfied, he pulled a ball of twine from his pocket and tied the tree into a cone shape for ease of transportation. He handed his tools over to Salter.

His new friend prevented Salter from cutting down either of the first two trees he stopped at—one was completely bare on one side and the other bent halfway up at an angle of forty-five degrees—and they agreed on a third one. Salter picked up the saw and found that he had not been watching the man closely enough. How had he got around the need to jam his face into the tree in order to get close enough to cut it? But Salter dived in, ignoring the strips being torn off his face by the branches because by now everyone was finished and watching him. Finally he stepped back from the fallen tree and moved to pick up the ax, but his friend gently interceded and quickly trimmed the tree for Salter, wrapped it, and handed him the end of the trunk to drag over to the trailer. When Salter had dumped it on to the flatbed he looked around for Seth, but the boy was holding a private conversation with the horse, as distant from his father as he could get.

The final ignominy was having to borrow some twine from his mentor to tie the tree to the roof rack of his car.

When they arrived home, Seth said to Annie in a sing-song voice, "Daddy didn't have a saw and another man had to help him."

Annie looked at Salter's face and said, "Well, you were right, dear. Sorry." She looked at the tree. "It's a lovely tree, Charlie. Don't worry about a stand. I'll get one next week. Oh, look, it's snowing."

Salter looked up and saw the first flakes to reach the city falling gently out of the sky. On the whole he was glad he had gone. He had saved himself as much as six dollars, and the tree his friend had selected was, indeed, straight. And his sense of injury was money in the bank to protect him from any suggestions from Annie for some days to come.

Chapter

5

"The only one I've talked to who knew her was this friend from the old days, and he hadn't seen her for the last three months, so he couldn't tell me much about her life in Toronto. He said her husband was old-fashioned and she wasn't, but I think he was just guessing about her." Salter was talking to his superintendent the next day.

"That why her husband kicked her out?"

"She left *him,* apparently, but yes, that was the reason. He did catch her once coming out of a motel with some guy."

"Who was that, do you know?"

"No. He didn't show up in the first investigation. I'll find out if I can. Maybe he can tell me what she was like."

"What are you trying to do, Salter? Build a psychological profile of the woman?" Orliff smiled.

"Yes, I am," Salter said defensively. "The FBI figures

that if they can get an accurate profile of the victim they can create an idea of the kind of person who killed her. If I get enough stuff, maybe I'll ask them what they think."

"Good luck," Orliff said skeptically. "So what are you going to do next?"

"I'm going to talk to these two guys she met through the ad, and then I'm going to Winnipeg. Talk to her husband and anyone else I can find."

Orliff flicked through the file and took out a sheet of paper. "According to this, the husband was at his cottage, but there are no witnesses to that. Could he have done it?"

"Probably not. His mother saw him on the Friday evening, and he was back on Sunday night. I'll check the flights again, just to make sure."

"According to the statement, he was planning to come to Toronto the following weekend to see her. It might be interesting to find out why, if he's telling the truth, that is. But you're right. He claimed the body for burial in Winnipeg, and the Winnipeg police think he was telling the truth to them."

"I'll see these guys this afternoon and then go to Winnipeg. Maybe I can talk to other people who knew her."

"Is this going to satisfy that old wife of yours, do you think?"

"I don't know." Salter shrugged. "She's coming by in about an hour. I can show her that we're doing it all twice. That should be enough."

"Don't forget, Salter. Don't get your hopes up. In my opinion this crime was committed by a flake who followed her home and waited in the hall. Right? Don't hope to catch him. Just demonstrate our efficiency."

"So. What have you found out?" Gerry took off her parka and sat down opposite him, dumping her big leather satchel on her lap.

Salter told her. He went through the story with a deliberation designed to impress her, emphasizing the door-to-door search that had been conducted for possible witnesses, and the elimination of all the men Nancy was known to have been in touch with. He added that he planned to go over the ground again, including seeing the husband in Winnipeg. "There look to be two possibilities," he concluded. "One, the obvious and mostly likely, is that she was the victim of a weirdo. The other one is that she was killed by someone she invited home for the night. Either way it's going to be hard to catch him, if not impossible."

She listened until he finished, but toward the end she was nodding acceptance of each point before he had finished making it, impatient to make a point herself.

"How promiscuous was she, Charlie? Did she sleep around with everybody?"

"I don't know yet. She was fairly new in town, and so far the only people I've spoken to who knew her are Mrs. Loomis and a guy who knew her in Winnipeg. Neither was much help. Why?"

"Would it make any difference?"

"Sure. If she slept with every guy she met, it will be hard to get a lead on him, won't it?"

"That isn't what I meant. But never mind. I thought it might matter to you so I made it my business to find out."

"You did *what*?"

"I made my own inquiries. Want to know what I learned?" She took a school exercise book out of her satchel and got ready to open it.

"Are you telling me that you've been snooping around investigating this thing yourself? Jesus Christ Almighty. What the hell do you think you're up to? Eh? What in bloody hell do you think you are doing? Did you pose as a cop, or what? Now look. This is a murder investigation, a *police* investigation. If you want to know anything, ask me. Otherwise stay out of the way, and if you don't like it, go see the mayor, or your political pals up at Queen's Park. But don't fart around playing the private eye. Okay?"

She waited until he had finished shouting, and then for several more seconds to indicate that she was not going to reply in kind. Then she said, "I didn't tell anyone I was a cop, private or otherwise. Nobody's interfering with your investigation."

"What *did* you tell them, whoever you talked to? Just so that I know when the complaints come in."

"Nothing that will cause you any problems. I talked to the women she worked with and a couple of others they put me on to. I didn't tell them I used to be married to you. I didn't even tell them it was Nancy Cowell

I was primarily interested in. Do you want to hear anymore?"

"Sure I do. I'd like to know everything you've been up to."

They stared at each other, waiting.

"Well?" Salter asked.

She waited for something else, then continued. "I told them I was a free-lance journalist, writing an article on the vulnerability of women. How's that? Nancy Cowell was just a name, I had lots of them, and I told them I wanted to know if she fitted into a pattern of the kind of women who got raped. Now, can I say something? I *have* done some free-lance journalism, and I *may* write an article on this yet, so what I'm doing is completely legitimate and if you don't like it, that's too bad, but I'm going to do it anyway. Now do you want to hear what I found out or not? Suit yourself."

"I told you," Salter said. "Let's hear it."

She opened her notebook. "I talked to three of the women she worked with," she repeated, "and these two others. I've got pages of notes here, but I'll give you a summary. From what they told me, Nancy Cowell was neither a shrinking violet nor a raging tart. She'd had some dates since she came to Toronto, but you don't get to meet many people—men, that is—possible dates, that is—in social work. So they often used to talk about how to meet eligible males. Two of these women associated themselves totally with Nancy. I mean, they used "we" a lot, they shared her interest in widening the circle. They'd all tried the singles bars but didn't like them, and one of them had advertised, too. She said she and Nancy decided together to put ads in the paper, as a kind of joke, but as she said, it would have been nice if they had worked. She lost her nerve when the replies came in, but Nancy went out with several of the men who wrote to her."

"I know. We have their names."

"The point I'm making is not that I was looking for suspects—that's your job—but that Nancy Cowell had whatever it takes to try to do something about her situation."

"And get killed in the process."

"No, I don't think so. Because one thing they were sure of, all of them, was that Nancy would never take someone home she wasn't certain of. They talked about this among themselves all the time, and they all agreed that it was a no-no. The fact is that Nancy was no different from any of these women, or thousands of others in Toronto, I guess. She didn't stroll around High Park at night, and she didn't take strangers home to bed."

"But after a few dates, yes, right?"

"Sure, I guess. She was free, wasn't she? But she was also fussy. Not moral, *fussy*. They used to joke about it. The impression I got was that she was a little hard to please. As far as they were aware, she wasn't having an affair, and they would have known if she was."

"But she was looking for a man."

"Sure she was. They all are. The right one."

The battle had died down now, and Salter had had time to realize that Gerry had saved him a great deal of work, and her results were probably reliable. "All right," he said. "Thanks. I wouldn't have been able to get so close to these people. So I'm not looking for a one-night stand. What about her husband? Did you find out anything about him, or him and her? I guess this wouldn't come into your article, eh?" Salter managed a half grin.

"We did talk about other stuff, off the record, when the interview was over."

"So you *did* do a little snooping?"

"It was interesting talking about her. Apparently she didn't mention her husband much. These women had the impression that she was still feeling protective of him, as if she was still married to him. She didn't talk much about Winnipeg, or why she broke up, although one girl remembered her making a remark about his being jealous. She went out a couple of times with a man, a friend from Winnipeg, but they didn't know who it was and she hadn't mentioned him for a long time."

"Her husband was coming to town that week after she was killed. Did she mention that to anybody?"

"No one said anything about it. She probably didn't want to discuss him."

"That it?" Salter asked, after a pause.

"Not quite. Once in the early days, before these women knew her very well, she came to work with a black eye. She wouldn't talk about it, so they suspected she had been punched out. All she said was, 'I ran into a lump of iron.' So what do you think? This week a black eye, next week strangled?"

But Salter evaded the question, working still to keep Gerry from feeling like an equal partner in the investigation. He waved a hand at the notebook. "Apart from the black eye, you didn't get anything much, did you?"

"No, I didn't. That's the point, though, isn't it? Whatever else you find out about her, she was normal, sensible, wary, and fussy."

"What are you getting at?"

She wriggled slightly in her chair and pulled the satchel close to her chest. "It's just that I was worried that you were thinking in categories. Was she a tart? Was she a nice girl? Stuff like that. Why wouldn't you? You've been out of the world for eighteen years, happily married. Have you ever been in a singles bar in your life?"

Salter ignored the question. "As a matter of fact, you've found out just what I wanted to know. You asked all the right questions for all the wrong reasons, but you've been a big help."

"What wrong reasons?"

"Trying to show how wrong I am," Salter said. "But I'm interested in her behavior patterns, not in judging her. I do the judging at home. Here I just want to find out who killed her."

"Sorry."

"That's all right. Just so you know." He collected himself to put a new question. "You can do something else for me, if you like." His encounter with Agnes Loomis had irritated him enough that he had neglected to go over one possibly important question, and he had been steeling himself to go back and ask it. Now maybe Gerry could do it for him.

"Agnes Loomis," he began. "She was the last person to speak to Cowell. Can you see if she remembers exactly what Cowell said when she called her that night? The record shows that she apologized for calling so late, and they arranged to meet at eight the next morning to go to the market. Then the transcript says that she was asked if Cowell said anything else about who she had been with, and Loomis said no. But try and find out exactly what words Nancy used, will you?"

"Sure. I'm seeing her this afternoon anyway. This might be a bit trickier, though. I may have to tell her I'm investigating it myself."

Salter shrugged. "Tell her what a bunch of assholes you think we are. That'll please her."

She laughed and stood up. "Now that we've cleared the air, can I ask you a question?"

Salter watched her doubtfully. "What if I say no?" he asked.

"What?"

"What if I say no? You mean personal, don't you? Yes, I am very happy with my wife, thank you."

She laughed and shook her head. "I'm sure you are. I'd like to meet her."

In a pig's ear, thought Salter. "What was your question?"

"Why did you marry me?"

"What?"

"You heard. Did you like me so much, or did I make it easy for you?"

"I wouldn't have asked you if I didn't like you, would I? And it was better to marry than burn, as they say."

"I liked you, too, and I made up my mind to have you. I still like you."

What was she up to? "Then why were you so goddamn determined to screw me up? You knew I couldn't put up with that stuff you started to get into. Possession of marijuana meant six months in jail in those days, and I was a cop when you married me, remember?"

"I remember, all right. I guess that was it. If you'd been a cab driver we might have made it, but I didn't like being Caesar's wife."

"What's that supposed to mean? I know what Caesar's wife is. Are you saying you're sorry we broke off? That was a long time ago. I haven't thought about you for years . . ." A little brutal talk would break that tiny web he thought she was spinning.

"No. I'm sorry we got married. It wasn't fair to you."

Salter shrugged. He didn't want her pity, either.

"Will you come home with me if I come to the office later on this afternoon?"

"What for?" Salter asked.

Her face went wry. "I'm not trying to seduce you, idiot. My sixteen-year-old son will be at home."

"Then what do you want me to come home with you for?" Salter persisted.

"For ten minutes, is all." She stood up. "It doesn't matter. I'll come by in a few days."

"I'm kind of busy," he said. "I have to report to the people you've been needling." Then, perversely, he said, "All right. Come by at five. I'll drop you off on the way home."

Two of the men who had responded to Cowell's ad were coming in later that afternoon, and Salter considered how to use the intervening time. He spent a few minutes brooding about his ex-wife's request. She wanted his good opinion about something, that was obvious, and Salter found it pleasant, if disturbing, that she still cared enough about his opinion to lay herself open to him. So why was he throwing up the barricades? He knew the answer, had known it since she first walked into his office and he had heard or felt along his nerves a tiny squeak of sexuality in their meetings, a pulse that beat less often in his relationships nowadays and was listened to with less interest when it did.

"What now?" Gatenby asked.

Salter looked at his watch. "I'm going down to talk to the O.P.P. I'll be back before those guys come in. Call Annie, would you, and tell her I may be a bit late."

The Ontario Provincial Police has its headquarters on Harbour Street, near the Lakeshore. Salter called ahead and was promised some time with an inspector who had recently transferred from the Kenora district in Northwest Ontario, an area that takes in Rat Portage.

Inspector Mordern was waiting for him when he arrived and took him into a small conference room where a map had been spread out on a table.

"I thought you'd like to see the problem," Mordern said. "After you called me, I talked to our boys in Kenora, and they explained what they had done. Actually most of it was done by the Winnipeg police, because that's where people with cottages in his area mostly live. Anyway, here's the story. This guy closed his cottage up after Labor Day, which means that there would be hardly anyone around. Everyone closes up on Labor Day except the fishermen, and they are generally closed up a week or so after. So almost no one was around that weekend, and when we went to check, there really *was* no one. Now, Kowalczyk's cottage is here, so we asked the owners of all the cottages that could see his—not too many because he's in a kind of channel—and drew a blank. We also asked at every point along the route. The marina confirmed that he had arrived early Friday afternoon and left on Sunday. We couldn't find any witnesses, but that's no surprise. People like that area because they can be alone there."

"How far is it to his cottage from Winnipeg?"

"Two hundred and ten kilometers. About a hundred and thirty miles."

"He filled up with gas before he left, and again on the Trans-Canada just before he hit Winnipeg on the way back. That fits, doesn't it? If he'd driven the road twice he would need more gas, and he didn't charge any more that weekend."

"If this thing was planned, it would be kind of elementary to pay cash for the other trip, wouldn't it?"

Salter sighed. "I know. How long would it take him to close up his cottage?"

"Probably a day's work. Depends."

Salter took Kowalczyk's original statement out of his pocket. "He had to put shutters up, drain the taps, and take his chain saws up to the marina so that no one would steal them during the winter; then he left his boat in the marina for storage and paddled his canoe back to his cottage."

"What then? Does he put the canoe on top of his car?"

"No. He stores it under the porch. Then, in the spring he drives into the cottage and paddles up to the marina to fetch his boat."

The O.P.P. inspector considered. "That sounds like a good day's work to me. I could have one of our guys check it out. They can still get in there with a snowmobile." He made a note. "How long, including the canoe trip, to close up?" he repeated. "That's a day, say, but he was up two days. What did he do on the second day?"

"He says he spent a day fishing."

"Did he catch anything?"

"He says he did, but he didn't bring anything back."

"Jesus. You'd think there would be something. Anyway, I'll have our guys check it out and I'll give you a call. What's this all about, anyway?"

"It's an open case, and we're getting some pressure. So I'm checking everything twice."

"They think you've been sitting on your hands?"

"That's the size of it. Thanks."

The first man answered Salter's questions readily enough. He was tall, bony, and slightly weatherbeaten, in a blue suit and black shoes with dark hair parted low on one side and combed flat on his skull. Arthur Schrader.

"According to your testimony, you met Nancy Cowell just once, Mr. Schrader?"

"Twice. I had a drink with her once, and I met her once more."

"When was the second time?"

"I took her to my club to play tennis. That was the last time."

"You didn't say anything about this before."

"I did, but the sergeant didn't think it was worth recording."

"I see. Where did you meet her the first time?"

"By arrangement, in a pub in the Eaton Centre. At least I found out then she was no gold digger, so we arranged to play tennis."

"I see. And why didn't you see her again?"

"Because she couldn't play tennis. She said she could, the first time, so I arranged a foursome with two of my friends. She absolutely let me down. A complete waste of time. Couldn't even serve properly."

"That's too bad. You were looking for a tennis partner, were you?"

"I was looking for someone compatible. I play tennis every night during the summer, and I belong to the Mayfair Club during the winter. I'm a very fair player, and I wanted someone who could share my interests."

"Didn't she have any other interests you could share?"

"I never found out. If she couldn't play tennis, she probably lied about the fact that she could play bridge, too! I wasn't going to take the chance of ruining any more of my friends' evenings."

"Did you ever sleep with her?"

"What?" Schrader seemed outraged. "You think I would go to bed with a woman on the first meeting? There's plenty of men who would, I know, and maybe that was what she wanted, but I'm not one of those, thank you. I like to be pretty sure of whom I'm with. Oh, no, Inspector, not me. I suppose I should have realized that women who put ads in the paper have that in mind, but she seemed quite nice that first time."

"You live with your sister, Mr. Schrader?"

"Yes, I do. And she can confirm where I was that night. I was at the club until just after nine, and then I came home and watched a bit of television. I went to bed early because I had arranged a game for seven the next morning."

"Thanks, Mr. Schrader. I won't bother you again."

"Good. It isn't very nice, you know. You answer an ad in all good faith, and suddenly the police think you're a rapist, or something. And now you're questioning me all over again."

"We have to question everybody. What I'm really looking for is some information, any information, that relates to Nancy Cowell's life-style. I assume she didn't say much about herself?"

"Nothing. She was a social worker, I know that, but I don't even know where she lived. She wanted to drive herself home and I didn't press her very hard because I wasn't going to see her again, and I had some apologies to make to my friends."

"Thanks, Mr. Schrader."

"Thank *you.*"

The second man was well over six feet tall; he moved awkwardly, as if the bones of his arms and legs fitted badly. He was wearing a flannel shirt, chino pants, Greb boots, a big army surplus parka; about forty-five with a slightly sea-dog air that was created by a coarse skin and a matted beard that needed trimming. He had a curious whining way of talking, like an old-time movie cowboy, as though in his twenties he had adopted a verbal slouch, a drawl, that came from the top of his nose. He posed in the chair on one buttock, leaning his face heavily on his hand, and looked quizzically at Salter from under his eyebrows.

Salter began. "According to your statement, Mr. Henning, you met Nancy Cowell only once, for a drink. Right?"

Henning fished a cigarette out of his pocket, lit it,

and held it between his teeth. Then he shook his head at Salter, took the cigarette out and slouched forward confidentially in his chair. "I took her out more than once," he said.

"So why did you say you didn't?"

"You ever been questioned, Inspector?" Henning was working hard to control the conversation, and Salter, for the moment, let him have his head.

"No, why?"

"Some of you guys can get real rough, you know? And the way your guys started in on me, I figured I might be in for a bad time. Cops like to make arrests, you know," he concluded, instructing Salter in the facts about the real world.

"Why didn't you ask for a lawyer? It says here you waived that."

"Hell, that's a sure sign, isn't it?"

"Let's start again. How well did you know her? How many times did you see her?"

Henning pulled his parka around him and sat up. He spread his left hand out to count. "First, when we set up the meeting. Second, we had a drink in Joe Bird's on Yonge Street. That's not far from where I work. Three: we had a bite to eat in the Pink Rose Café on Spadina, a hamburger, and just sat and talked."

"Why didn't you see her again?"

"There wasn't time, was there? She was dead."

"What were you doing the night she got killed?"

"I made myself some supper, watched a little television, then went to work around ten."

All this checked with his earlier statement, and he had certainly been at work when Cowell was killed.

"Did you ever have relations with her?" Salter asked.

Henning looked at Salter as if about to challenge him, to make him eat his words.

"Were you ever intimate with her?" Salter repeated.

The pose broke and Henning shook his head. "No, I wasn't," he said.

"Why not?"

"Because she wasn't that kind."

"Did you expect to?"

"I expected to," Henning replied, "But she was no one-night stand."

"Were you ever in her apartment?"

Now the man stopped acting, and answered directly. "I didn't even know where she lived," he said.

"You met by arrangement, then? You phoned her?"

"No, we arranged that she would phone me. She didn't give out telephone numbers, either."

"Are you married?" Salter asked him suddenly.

Henning's face cleared. "I'm divorced. Nancy knew that because I told her."

So there was no obvious private guilt.

"Did you tell anyone, friends or people at work, that you met her through an ad?"

"Why should I? It's none of their goddamn business."

That was probably it. The man was afraid that if the police followed him up too hard then someone at work would hear about it, and that would spoil his image. The case had been intensively reported in the press, along with the story of the advertisement, and working where he did, the man was terrified that his co-workers would find out how he got his women.

"I'm trying to build up a profile of Nancy Cowell," Salter said. "From what you knew, would you go along with my opinion that she wasn't promiscuous, that she was lonely, but she might have gone to bed with the right guy, once she knew him well enough . . . ?"

Gratefully, Henning leaped. "You've got it in one. I'm sure, Inspector. She wouldn't screw around with anybody, but she was a real woman for the right guy. Yeah. That was what I liked about her. And that's okay with me, too." He tried a joke. "Anyway, what the hell, with all this herpes and stuff, lovin' has got kinda complicated again, hasn't it?" Henning rolled around in his chair to show he felt at home.

Salter allowed him to go without letting him off the hook entirely. He needed more confirmation of his own guess as to why Henning was unhappy. "Okay, Mr. Henning. Thanks for your cooperation. I'll be in touch again."

Gatenby appeared with the look of a man who has found something. "I've got a lady to see you, Charlie," he said.

"What for?"

Gatenby smiled. "Can I bring her in?" he asked.

"What are you up to, Frank? Is she selling something?"

"No, she's giving it away. I think she can find the third man for you."

"What are you talking about?"

"You know, the guy with no address. She can help us."

"Oh. All right, bring her in."

Gatenby grinned and disappeared to collect his witness.

The woman Gatenby ushered into the room entered with the pleased look of someone expecting a prize. A fur coat, heavily enameled makeup, dark glasses, and well-dyed fair-gray hair gave her the look of someone who always put her best face forward. Slightly tarty, thought Salter. Smells nice, too. About forty-five, he guessed, maybe fifty.

"This is Miss Leavis," Gatenby said.

"What can I do for you, Inspector?" she asked. "Besides suggest a new color scheme for your office. They don't do you very well here, do they?" An English accent and the small voice of someone who expects people to listen and lean if they want to hear her, accompanied by a companionable, slightly conspiratorial smile, as if she and Salter had found each other at last in a room full of strangers.

"I don't know," Salter said. "What can Miss Leavis do for us, Sergeant?"

"I think she may be able to identify our missing man," Gatenby said. "Show her the letter, sir."

Still wondering, Salter passed the anonymous letter over the desk.

She took her sunglasses off, replaced them with a pair of reading glasses that made her look slightly endearing, read the letter, then took a folded letter from her purse and spread it out beside Salter's letter. "I don't think there's much doubt," she said. "Look."

The two letters were nearly identical, and the handwriting was the same, but clipped to the woman's letter was a card, identifying the writer as Lionel Atterbury, Insurance Agent, with two telephone numbers.

"Where did you get this?" Salter asked.

"Through the post," she said with a little laugh. She put her glasses away and looked at Gatenby for guidance.

"The mail," Gatenby explained to Salter. "Miss Leavis put an ad in like the one we're investigating, with the same sort of wording, on the same day. So I called her and asked her what sort of replies she got. She was very happy to come along and talk to us."

"Exciting," the woman murmured. "Clever old duck, your sergeant."

Isn't he, thought Salter. "Would you have a look at these?" he asked, pushing over the letters of the two men he had questioned.

She glanced at the first and broke into another little trill of laughter. "The tennis man," she said. "Did you meet him?"

"Yes," Salter said. "Did you?"

"Only once. We met in this awful pub in the Eaton Centre and he asked me what my hobbies were. I stayed only a few minutes."

"And this one," Salter said, pointing to the letter from Henning.

"I thought he was rather nice," she said immediately. "But he wasn't really my type. I think he was poor, too. Probably paying support to his wife."

"Did he seem—" Salter searched for the word "—normal to you?"

"You're looking for someone kinky, aren't you, Inspector? Did some poor girl get assaulted by one of these men?"

"Yes," Salter said. "A woman was killed, but not necessarily by one of these."

"I'd lay my life on it," she said. "You can always tell. The tennis player was totally harmless, and this one, well, a bit sad, really, but not a sex maniac, not a bit of it. We had a nice drink, and he was easy enough to get along with but I never called him back. He needed someone else."

"And this one? The insurance agent?"

"Him I'm not *so* sure of. His letter was all right, and he took me to a nice bar, but he couldn't wait to get to the point."

"You mean he propositioned you right away?"

"No, no. But you could tell. Lots of remarks, sort of testing me out."

"Could you give me an example?"

"Oh, no. Just call it innuendo."

"What did you expect from an ad?" Salter asked. "Just curious, Miss Leavis, but what were you hoping to find?"

"I don't know. I thought perhaps I might snag someone I liked. Bit of a lark, really."

"Did you have any luck?"

"That's for me to know and you to find out, isn't it?" She laughed again. "No, I didn't. But it was quite fun in a way. Some of the letters were very sad, though."

"Thanks, Miss Leavis. I'll keep your letter, if you don't mind."

"If you want my advice, you won't bother. What kind of girl was she? I mean, had she been around, met a lot of men before?"

"I think she had led a pretty normal life."

"Then I think she would have known this Atterbury chap as quickly as I did. Any woman would."

When she had left, Salter said, "There goes a reliable witness as far as men are concerned, wouldn't you say, Frank?"

"I think she'd soon find out what you had in the bank," Gatenby said. "Still, if you did have a lot of money, she'd be all right, wouldn't she?"

"Don't dream. Get hold of this guy and bring him in." Salter put the file away. "You're a clever bastard, Frank, for finding her. I'll mention you in dispatches. Now I have to see my ex-wife."

"I think she's waiting for you," Gatenby said. "Shall I tell her you're coming out?"

"Okay. I think I'll go to Winnipeg the day after tomorrow, by the way. I may stay over. I'll call you. And dig those passenger lists out, will you? I want to look at them before I go."

. . .

"I live on Lonsdale," Gerry said. "At Spadina."

Salter drove across to Spadina Avenue, then followed the road north. "I'm still in the dark about why you want me to go home with you," he said once they had settled into the stream of traffic.

"Are you nervous?"

"I'm curious. Am I going to meet your new boyfriend or lover or what?"

"Nothing like that. You're going to see my apartment, that's all."

"Why? You proud of the decoration?"

"Yes, if you like. I asked Agnes Loomis about the phone call. What did you think of her, by the way?"

"About what I expected. So goddamn busy looking after the world she hasn't time to cook a meal for her kids."

"A real Mrs. Jellyby, eh?"

"A what?"

Gerry explained: Mrs. Jellyby, Dickens's famous portrait of the original concerned woman, who spent all her time worrying about the starving Africans while her own children suffered.

"That's about it. The house was a mess, too."

They were crossing Bloor now, where the avenue became Spadina Road.

"Dirty, was it?"

"A mess," Salter said. "And no food in the house."

"Did the kids look underfed? Were they in rags?"

Now Salter heard the warning bells. "I guess not," he said. "What's this all about?"

"Agnes told me. You caught her at a bad time."

"I'll say I did. Drinking tea like cat's piss and serving the worst cookies I've ever eaten."

Gerry shrugged. "She was having an off day."

"Was that it? They were planning on hot dogs for dinner. Again, the kid said. It sounded like a pretty typical day to me. If that's the counterculture or alternate life-style or whatever you call it, you can have it."

"Okay, so it isn't the way you'd like to live. But don't generalize about it. There are plenty of lousy housekeepers in Etobicoke, too."

"Sure, but everyone knows what they are—sluts. Too busy watching game shows all day to cook dinner. What's the difference? Agnes Loomis is too busy saving the goddamn world. That's all. Why do you think her husband left?"

Gerry stayed silent as they reached Lonsdale, and Salter found a place to park near her apartment block. They climbed the stairs to her apartment on the second floor in silence. The block, and her apartment, were of a type fast disappearing in Toronto. Terrazzo floors and old oak woodwork led to a solid front door. Inside, through a tiny hall, lay a two-bedroom apartment that contained a real dining room as well as a glass-enclosed sun porch. The place was furnished in what Salter thought of as homespun—rag rugs, colored blankets on the couches, and wooden objects; old bread molds and badly carved ducks in flight—on the walls. In the kitchen, where Gerry now led him, Salter had the sense of dozens of containers and implements, a place that was in constant use. Gerry turned on the heat under a pot of water and took a small saucepan out of the refrigerator and put it on the stove. She lifted two bottles of beer inquiringly; Salter nodded, and she found glasses. Before she sat down, she called through to the end of the apartment and a boy of about sixteen appeared in the doorway.

"Joe, I'd like you to meet Mr. Salter," she said. "I'm trying to help him with that murder I told you about."

The boy came forward and shook hands. "How do you do, sir," he said. Then, to his mother, "How long? I have hockey practice."

"Ten minutes. You might as well stay. Sit down and talk to the inspector."

Salter grubbed around for an opening. "I hear you want to join us?" he said. He found himself, absurdly, examining the boy for some resemblance to himself.

"No, sir. The Mounties."

"Why?"

"I want to go up north, to the Yukon. But I've always wanted to be a Mountie."

"Don't most of them stand around looking pretty for the tourists in Ottawa?" Salter teased.

"No, they don't," the boy said with a hint of belligerence. "Most of them are on provincial police duty. That's what I want to do."

Gerry had dropped spaghetti into the boiling water, set out a placemat, napkin, and cutlery for the boy, and sliced some bread off a round Italian loaf. When the spaghetti was cooked, she served it with a sauce unfamiliar to Salter, pale with bits of ham in it, and set down a dish of grated cheese. As soon as he started eating she fixed a salad out of ingredients that were washed and ready, and set out a piece of apple cake and a glass of milk.

"Let's go in the other room and leave Joe alone," she said.

"I'd like to hear the inspector questioning you," Joe said.

Screw this, Salter thought. He found himself offended by the boy's manner to his mother, which seemed to Salter to lack courtesy or affection. "I don't have any questions," he said. "I've asked them all. I just dropped your mother off on my way home."

Joe looked sharply at his mother. Then to Salter he said, "I know who you are."

"Do you? Good. It's nice to meet you," Salter said and finished his beer. He got up to go, and Gerry walked him to the door and down the stairs.

"You just wanted to show him your first husband?" Salter asked when they reached the door.

"That's what Joe thinks. What do you think?"

"I don't know. You wanted me to see him?"

"That's what I wanted you to see. Not him, but him being all right. You thought I would be living in some rathole, didn't you, full of hippies sleeping three to a bed. Or maybe Mrs. Jellyby's."

"Why should I think that?" Salter protested.

She laughed and leaned forward to kiss him on the cheek. "It was written all over your face. Another thing.

Joe is my chaperone. I lead a very quiet life. Now go home to Annie."

"What did Mrs. Jellyby say, by the way?" Salter asked.

"Oh, God, yes. Hold on." She disappeared inside the apartment and reappeared with her notebook. "Here it is," she said. "Ready? Nancy: Hi, Agnes. Sorry to be calling so late, but I've been out. Okay for the market tomorrow? Eight o'clock? Agnes: Sure thing. Where did you go? Nancy: I'll tell you all about it tomorrow. We got soaked coming home and I've got to hang up my clothes properly."

"That all?" Salter asked.

"That's it. Agnes swears it's word for word. It's something, isn't it? 'We' means she came home with someone, and according to my informants, someone she knew well enough to trust."

"Sure, but what does 'home' mean? To the front door? But you may be right. Thanks."

It was much later, in thinking about the case after it was over, that he realized it was Loomis's account of the last phone call which had stuck in his head and become the real starting point of the final trail.

That evening, when Salter told Annie about his adventure, she said, "She wanted to show you off to the boy, too."

"You mean she's proud of us? Both of us? I thought he was a bit of a lout, myself. And he didn't seem to like his mother much."

"I didn't say that. I mean she knew he would approve

of you, and you would approve of the way she lives. I'd like to meet her."

"I'll invite her for Christmas, shall I?"

"Don't be silly, Charlie."

Nevertheless he wondered what his first wife did at Christmas, and being fiercely sentimental about it himself, he hoped she had somewhere to go.

The next morning he had been in the office for an hour when the call came through from the O.P.P. inspector.

"Interesting little development," the inspector said. "I don't know what it means, but there's no canoe under the porch. Everything else checks out, though. They say that it would have been at least a day's work to close the cottage and paddle back from the marina. The guy at the marina says he thinks he remembers Kowalczyk paddling back, but he's not sure. That any help?"

"I'm not sure that it makes a lot of difference. As far as I can see, it just means that he had a few extra hours to play with. That would help some, but not much."

"Anything else I can do?"

"Yes. Find me someone who took a picture of him outside his cottage on Saturday morning."

"Or at the airport."

"Right. Thanks anyway."

Salter put the phone down and went back to studying the passenger lists that Gatenby had put on his desk. On the crucial one, the Friday flight, every name but two had been checked off, and there was a notation that those two, a man and a woman, were unlocatable.

"What name would you use if you were traveling incognito, Frank?" Salter asked.

"Orliff," Gatenby said promptly.

Salter laughed. "Why?"

"It's the first one that comes to mind after John Smith," he said. "And it sounds authentic."

"Yeah," Salter agreed. He made a note of the two names of the unidentified passengers. "Now I have to talk to the real Orliff," he said.

"What do you think, Salter? Give it back to Wycke?" Orliff suggested.

"No. Let me think about it. I need to check on this canoe and then he can have it."

"How will you do that?"

"I'm going to ask the husband if he can explain the canoe. I'll fly down tomorrow."

"To Winnipeg? Jesus, Salter, that's expensive. Why don't you phone Winnipeg and have them do it?"

"I want to get a look at the guy. And a couple of other people there. Just so I can say I've checked."

"I'll tell you what he'll say. 'Someone stole it.' Okay, but watch it, will you? Money's getting tight."

"I'll take some sandwiches to eat in my room," Salter promised.

Chapter

6

Salter had visited Winnipeg once before, at the end of a summer when he had worked in the bush in Northern Ontario after dropping out of university. With a pocketful of money saved from the summer, he had spent a few vivid days in a hotel on Main Street near the Canadian Pacific Railway station. Here he had been adopted by a group of plumbers on leave from a construction job in the Arctic. They had taken over one floor of the hotel, laid in a stock of rye whiskey, Chinese food, and local girls, and invited Salter to help himself. "The kid," they called him, giving him a mascotlike status when they intercepted him on his way to his room one night, just as the party was getting going. "Let the kid by," one of them said as Salter tried to step over two men who were lying in the corridor drinking beer and playing blackjack. Then, "Hey, kid, you on your own?" they asked. "Join the party." So he spent the next two days in a drunken haze, not quite sure afterward which parts of the party he had been involved in and which he had just been watching. He fell asleep at one point, luckily in his own room, for when he woke the police were just breaking things up. He dressed, retrieved his wallet from under the mattress, and moved to the Marlborough Hotel and a quieter life.

Now he checked into the Marlborough Hotel once more and walked out to Portage Avenue to see if he recognized anything. He got as far as the corner of Portage and Main, intending to walk along Main Street for a few blocks, but the wind that was roaring down Portage Avenue turned left with him along Main Street and in a very few minutes he was so cold he hailed a cab to police headquarters, where he was expected. This was no more than a courtesy call to acknowledge that he was working in someone else's territory, and he turned down the offer of a car and driver for the rest of his calls, preferring to function with as low a profile as possible.

He took a cab from the headquarters to Kowalczyk's house on Inkster Boulevard, where he found, as he expected, that Victor Kowalczyk was at work, and asked for some time with Mrs. Cowell, his mother, who apparently kept house for him.

She was a big woman with a slightly battered face that wore the expression of someone who expected to have to fight for what was hers. She admitted Salter into the living room and offered him coffee, which he accepted to give him time to look around. The room and its furnishings were foreign to Salter, equally alien both to his home with Annie and the Anglo-Saxon ghetto of his childhood. The strangeness began with the smell: unfamiliar foods had been cooked in this place, and their presence lay under the odor of furniture polish and bleach with which Mrs. Cowell had been punishing the apartment. The furniture was a mixture: Salter sat in an armchair facing an old black upright chair which, he guessed, predated Mrs. Cowell. Fawn-colored broadloom was overlaid with a few small dark rugs that were slightly threadbare. Every ledge and table was loaded with framed photographs and ornaments that were there for their own sake, not to complement each other or the room, but to fill it with the familiar.

Mrs. Cowell brought him his coffee and seated herself in the upright chair. She waited for him to speak.

Salter cleared his throat. "We are still investigating the death of your daughter-in-law, Nancy Cowell," he said, and was cut off immediately.

"You should forget about her," Mrs. Cowell said. The accent was thick, the voice heavy.

"You didn't like her?"

"She gave my Victor a very bad time. It's true even if she is dead."

"She was unfaithful to your son?"

"She slept with everybody, before she is married and after."

"How do you know?"

"Everybody knows."

"Did your son know?"

"No, no. She acted like a nice girl, but I know her

kind. I didn't want Victor to marry her because she was not like Victor thought. Then he found out himself."

"At the motel?"

"Yes."

"Who told him where she was?"

"He got a phone call. So he went to see."

"Who called? Who made the call?"

"We never know. But it was true."

"So he got a phone call. Anything else?"

"Sure. I told you."

Salter saw little point in continuing. He had established that Mrs. Cowell spoke out of an iron prejudice against her daughter-in-law, and that her opinion on most things connected to the case would therefore probably be useless.

One more, just for the record. "Your son was at the cottage that weekend, I believe," he said.

"Yes."

"Did you see him on the Friday before he left?"

"Sure. I made early supper for Victor and Adela before they went off."

"Your daughter? Does she live with you?"

"No. She has her own apartment. But she came to supper on Friday instead of Sunday, like Victor. She went to Dauphin for the weekend to see my sister and her cousins. My sister's husband has a big farm in Dauphin."

"And your son came back on Sunday night. Right?"

"Yes."

Salter finished his coffee and stood up. "Do you have your daughter's phone number?" he asked.

"She is working now. Why? Why do you bother her?"

"I just want to talk to her for a few minutes. Do you have her number at work?"

Mrs. Cowell read out the number from a list by the telephone. "She is at the university," she said. "She is head of the laboratory."

"What time does your son get home?"

"I don't know. Victor is very busy. Maybe seven o'clock."

"Where is he working today?"

"In his office. He is a partner in a building company. Why do you have to upset him again?"

"Because I have to. What's his number?"

Reluctantly Mrs. Cowell gave it to him. He put his coat on and moved to the door.

"You think you can find him from all the men she was with?" she asked.

"Probably not, but I have to look. Thanks, Mrs. Cowell."

He walked along Inkster Boulevard looking for a cab. He found one outside a drugstore, the driver fast asleep, and asked him to wait while he called the daughter. When she came to the phone, he learned she was expecting him. Mrs. Cowell had already phoned to warn her.

"What do you want to talk to me about?" she asked.

"I want to talk to people who knew Nancy Cowell in

Winnipeg," he said. "You probably saw a lot of her. Can I have half an hour?"

"All right. I'll go to lunch early. Pick me up in three-quarters of an hour. It'll take you most of that to get here and find me." She gave him the name of the building she worked in.

Salter signaled to the cabbie to wait some more, whereupon the cabbie pointed to his meter, threw up his hands and made a performance of taking another nap. Salter called Victor Kowalczyk and found him in his office, also forewarned of Salter's visit, and prepared to meet him in the afternoon.

"The university," Salter said, getting in the cab.

"Which one?"

Salter was surprised at the question. "It's half an hour away," he said.

"That's the University of Manitoba, out at Fort Garry," the driver said.

"Good, let's go."

"There's two universities, y'see. There's the University of Winnipeg, too."

"Manitoba is what I want."

"Three, maybe. I think the one in St. Boniface is a university now, too. Maybe not."

"Let's go to the University of Manitoba."

"Your decision, chief. I mean, you ask me for the university, I don't know which one you mean. It'll cost you ten bucks. If it's the wrong one, it'll cost you another ten to get back downtown."

"Let me waste my money, will you? Let's go."

"If you say so." Finally the cabbie engaged his gears and they took off.

He punctuated the ride down the Pembina Highway by pointing to his meter every time it rang up another dollar. When he reached a bus stop on the campus, he stopped. "Which building?" he asked. "This is a ginormous campus."

"It just looks that way until you've seen Paree," Salter said. "The Agriculture Engineering building."

"Where's that at?"

"Oh, for Christ's sake." Salter rolled down his window and got directions from a passing student. When they pulled up in front of the building the fare was nine dollars. Salter gave the cabbie ten and asked for a receipt.

"Ah," the cabbie said. "You're on expenses. You don't give a shit. Right? You from the States?"

"Yes," Salter said. "How did you guess?"

Adela Cowell's face was round and her eyes narrow, and she emphasized this slightly oriental look by cutting her straight black hair square around her jaw. She suggested that they drive back to the highway in her car to a motel coffee shop where they would be away from her colleagues.

"Why are you going over this again?" she asked when they had their sandwiches and coffee in front of them. "Have you got a new theory?"

Salter shook his head. "Nope," he said. "Some pressure from above to take a second look. The usual reason."

She frowned. "Who cares?" she asked. "Who cares? Nancy had no other relatives, and Victor just wants to forget it."

"My first wife cares," Salter said, and told her the story of his own involvement. He was surprised to find himself telling her this, but he needed her confidence if he was to get beyond the routine questions. For her part, she was slightly confused by the sudden intimacy of his reply, and then she smiled, and Salter guessed it had been a good move.

"That's not the official answer," he concluded.

"I guess not, but it helps to know how the world works, doesn't it? Your first wife must be quite a woman."

Salter said nothing. He had laid himself open, and it was her move.

"What do you want to know?" she asked.

"I want to know what kind of woman Nancy Cowell was. I'd like to know privately, off the record, what you thought of her." In fact, Salter had fully accepted Gerry's assessment, but now he was circling his real interest, and a direct approach would almost certainly meet a blank wall in Adela Cowell.

"In what way?" She was stalling, waiting for a further sign that it was safe to relax. "Why?"

"Let's take two extremes," Salter said. "Or maybe three. On the one hand, if she was an easy mark, if she went to bed with every man she met, then the case is probably hopeless. Whoever did it might have met her the night before in a bar, and she took him home that night. On the other hand, if she was more discriminating than that, then whoever killed her knew her a little better, and we might have some chance of finding him."

"And the third?"

Salter sighed. "That's the one we usually come up with. She was killed by a weirdo, a drifter maybe, who got inside her apartment somehow and that was that. What bothers me about it is that she was killed quite late at night, when she would have been wary of opening the door to some stranger. And there was no sign of a forced entry. From that, I have to assume that she knew the guy slightly at least, or it's not worth bothering. Nice girls wait a while, even these days, don't they?"

The woman gave him a small ironic smile. "So they tell me," she said.

"What does that mean?"

"It means that it's a loaded question. I don't know what other people do."

"Okay, but her husband did see her coming out of a motel one afternoon with a man, didn't he?"

She nodded. "That's what split them up finally. But they had been in trouble for some time before that."

"Who was the guy?"

"No. Off the record, I know who he is, but I'm not going to tell you, because I don't trust you that far. He's getting married. If we go on the record, I'll say I don't know. It doesn't matter anyway. She didn't deny it."

"Did your brother know who he was? I'm going to ask him later."

"Ask him then."

"Does your brother still blame her?"

The woman sat back and pulled her jacket over her chest. "Ask him," she said. Then she slid forward on the bench and planted her wrists on the table. "Okay, I'll tell you if you'll understand that this is not to be used on Victor. If you want to use it you'll have to ask Victor about him first, and he's still very confused about it. When he first got the story he believed it the way it looked and he had my mother saying 'You see, you see' in his ear all the time. He heard enough from the police about those letters and the dating scene and all the rest of it so that he believed then, like you guys, that she was running around fast and loose and that one of her partners killed her for kicks, served her right. But there was other stuff going on. He couldn't shut my mother up, but I know he kept hoping that it was all wrong, that someday someone—you, maybe—would come along and prove otherwise. That's why he claimed Nancy's body and buried her here."

"What other stuff?"

Now the woman pulled her body into an even tighter protective hunch as she made her decision. "This is my mother we're talking about. Okay? I don't chat about this to everyone I meet, and you are going to forget it. I'm just telling you so it will modify your official attitude to Nancy, which you seem to want to do, just in case you can find the guy, and just in case, when you do,

Victor can sleep easier. I'll deny every goddamn word if you try it on officially."

Salter waited.

"Okay?" she demanded.

"If you tell me anything crucial, I may have to ask you officially."

"What I'm going to tell you is in answer to your question about what kind of person she was. It won't help you with your job, except to make you keep looking. It's not a clue."

"All right."

With her arms still folded around her upper body, she began. "You know that Vic was planning to visit her in Toronto the weekend after she was killed, don't you?"

"He said so in his original statement. He said they were going to meet to sort out their affairs."

"Yes, I told him to say that. He wouldn't have said anything about it, but you people already knew from someone in Toronto."

Salter nodded.

"He was hoping to get back together with her," she said.

"Why didn't he say so?" Salter asked. This must be the letter Tranby had talked about.

"Because he would have had to tell you a little family story that isn't very nice, and with Nancy dead, it no longer mattered. She had written to him, more than once apparently, asking him to come to Toronto, but he never got the letters because my mother threw them away."

"How do you know?"

"I don't. I guessed. It would be nice to say that I found the pieces of one in mother's garbage, but I didn't. Nancy phoned me and asked me if there was any way I could persuade my brother to reply to her letters, so I made it my business to find out that he had never received any letters from her. We didn't have a big confrontation or anything like that. I just called Nancy and told her to write to Vic at his office. So she did, and Vic called her and arranged to go to Toronto. Then she got killed."

"Why would your mother do this, if she did?"

"To save her son. Vic is her baby and she knew that Nancy was an evil witch, out to ruin her son's happiness, so she threw them away before Vic could see them."

"Thanks. Does your brother know what your mother was doing?"

"Not really. All he knows is that Nancy sent him a letter through his office. He thought it was strange, but I told him that Nancy was probably only thinking of saving him from being interrogated by mother. That satisfied him."

"You were on her side, were you? Nancy's, I mean."

She shrugged. "Not really. I was on Vic's side, and if he wanted her, that was all right with me."

"Didn't you get along with Nancy?"

"Sure, but we weren't friends. Vic shouldn't have married her in the first place. That's what I think now, anyway. But I liked her well enough," she added.

"In spite of what you knew about her?"

"What? What did I know about her? So she had an affair. So she should wear a big 'A' on her chest?"

"She had enemies though, didn't she? Or your brother did. What about the anonymous phone call?"

"Christ, I don't know. Some guy oozing slime over the wires. I told Vic to ignore it but he couldn't. He was born jealous, and mother had never stopped asking questions whenever Nancy was away for a day. She believed everything because she suspected it all along. Then Vic caught her at the motel."

"Which motel?"

She laughed. "This one right here." She pointed upward.

"She *was* having an affair, then?"

"Yes, I guess she was. And for Vic that was a very big deal. I think she loved Vic, though. So don't ask me why she was having an affair. I don't know. It is possible to love two people, you know. But she wasn't a tart and the guy who killed her must have been someone she was used to, not a one-night stand, so you've got your answer."

"Not really. He might have been a one-night stand who found out *she* wasn't and got mad."

She shook her head. "Whenever you say 'yes' for the first time, you wonder if this is the one who will turn into the Boston Strangler when you get home. But you can *nearly* always tell. You get signals, and she wasn't a kid. She would have picked up on a weirdo."

"She didn't have a lot of experience, though, did she? She married pretty young."

Adela blushed. "Not like me, you mean? You're probably right. But what I'm talking about you can learn in college."

They had finished eating, and Salter looked at the check. "I talked to Raymond Tranby in Toronto," he said. "You know him?"

She started to button her coat. "Sure. He was Vic's best friend. Still is, I guess. He knew Vic and Nancy as well as anybody. What did he say?"

"He was very helpful. He explained that for your brother, Nancy was a kind of Daisy Buchanan. You know? *The Great Gatsby.*"

Adela received this information with a small frown, and thought about it for a few moments. "What's that supposed to mean?" she asked. Then, quietly at first, but with increasing hostility, she continued. "Did he mean that Vic is the hunkie whose father 'et like a hog'? And who is Tranby in this scenario? Nick Carraway? Patronizing bastard. Jesus Christ. Where the hell does Tranby get off dreaming up fancy theories about my brother? That's *ridiculous.* You know what Tranby's father was? He was a court bailiff. Worked for the sheriff's court. His family rented out rooms on Maple Avenue. Did he tell you that?"

"He said that his grandfather was in the grain business with Nancy's grandfather."

"His grandfather was a clerk in a grain-company office downtown. Nancy's grandfather was a broker."

She's protesting a lot, thought Salter. "He was just trying to help a dumb cop understand the situation."

"Was he? Well, what he was giving you was a bit of Anglo mythology, Mr. Salter, about fifty years out of date, like *The Great Gatsby.* Nobody in hunkie-land yearns after your world anymore, if they ever did."

"It wasn't any ethnic thing he was talking about, but the poor boy/rich girl fairy story," Salter said.

"I know what he was talking about. Goddamn Anglo legends that go back to the Depression."

"Can I tell you a story?" Salter asked.

She stared at him, waiting.

"When I was a kid, twenty-five years ago, I went to a dance in Kenora one summer. I picked up a girl and we went back to the summer cabin she and two of her girl friends were renting for their vacation. We had a beer and got talking and I asked her what her name was, her last name. You know what she said?"

Adela Cowell watched him in silence.

"She told me her name. I've forgotten it now, and then she said, 'I'm Ukrainian. You don't mind, do you?' "

"So what did you say? 'I like Ukrainians,' and then you tried to jump her? What's that supposed to prove? Some little kid from an ignorant family with her eyes full of the big handsome Anglo—some kid who's been jeered at by the local slum Anglo creeps who thinks you may be different. It wouldn't happen nowadays, even with a girl like that. How old was she anyway? Fifteen? Listen, my mother raised us to be proud of ourselves. Tranby is full of crap."

"But your brother changed the family name?"

She looked furious and frustrated. "Yes, and Vic has changed it back. My older brother belonged to the fifties, like you, I suspect, but that's history now. Those days are gone. And Vic fell in love with Nancy Catchpole, not some goddamn Daisy. And the prejudice was all on our side, remember, starting with my mother. You need another novel."

"Look, I'll say it again. Tranby never mentioned the ethnic thing. You're jumping on this too hard."

"He didn't have to. I know what he was talking about. Okay. You want to know about us? I don't remember much about my father. He was twenty years older than my mother and he worked all the time, sixteen hours a day if he could. He came over from the Ukraine around nineteen-twenty and he worked all day as a construction laborer and at night building his house. He bought an old house for almost nothing and rebuilt it in his spare time, and when he got it finished, my mother took in boarders. He never spoke much English but he was reliable, so he got to be labor foreman for a plumbing and steam-fitting company. He was in charge of the gang who laid pipes in ditches ready for the welders."

"Tranby said he was killed when a tunnel collapsed."

She shook her head. "It wasn't a tunnel, it was a ditch. The shoring that was holding up the sides gave way and he was buried. He was working by himself, putting tar on the joints or something, and no one noticed until it was too late. There was a little bit of compensation and my brother got to go to law school, which was what Dad was working for. He believed in hard work, get ahead, you know? He wouldn't have anything to do with unions. An ideal company man—loyal, hard-working, all those things. I don't think his mates liked him much. He didn't have any friends that I know of—just us, his family. Work, work, work, save, save, save, don't answer back, keep your nose clean, put the kids through college. That was him."

Salter heard the note of judgment in her voice. "You think he was wrong?" he asked.

"I think we would have got into some arguments if he had lived. But it worked, didn't it? We all went to college like he planned. My brother is a big lawyer in Calgary, a wheeler-dealer in corporate law. And Victor's a partner in one of the biggest development companies in western Canada." Then she smiled. "And Vic's all right. You know why he changed his name back?"

"National pride?"

"No. In memory of his father. Family pride."

"But you didn't change your name back."

"No. Not yet, anyway. I don't care that much. I don't know." She shrugged the problem away. "So now you know about us. Vic married Nancy, not some Daisy-dream. Okay? Tranby's full of crap. Did Tranby tell you Victor wanted to offer him a job the last time he was between engagements?"

"No. What happened?"

"Vic's partners wouldn't have him. They said he had a bad name for getting up the backs of the architects and contractors. So now Vic's staking him in Toronto. If it wasn't for Vic, he'd be an office boy."

"He doesn't dress like an office boy."

"You noticed that? You know, I think he's just a fantastic snob who is waiting for us to recognize his natural superiority. He'll wait a long time." She pulled her woolen hat over her ears, tucking in her hair. "What happened to the little girl in Kenora, by the way?"

"What do you mean?"

"What did you do after she apologized for her race?"

"Nothing. I was embarrassed, and her friends came home right after that and I took off. I haven't thought about it since, until we started talking."

"I wonder what she thought of that," Adela said. She looked at her watch. "Now I have to go. Is that it? No more questions?"

There was a second level Salter wanted to get to, but he needed more time.

"Will you have dinner with me tonight?" he asked.

"You mean, like, you and me?" She looked at him bewildered. "A date, like?" she asked.

"Call it what you like. I'm staying over tonight and I don't like eating alone. I'd like to hear some more about Nancy."

She laced her fingers together and looked at Salter's tie, considering. "It's a bit unorthodox, isn't it?"

"Every case is different," Salter joked.

"Hmmm," she said. "Hmmm. Hmmm. Okay. Sure. I guess so. Sure. Why not? I guess I can trust you, can't I? Where?"

"Where is a good place? The only place I know is Rae and Jerry's."

She roared with laughter. "I *knew* you were going to say that. Did all you guys take your dates there in the fifties? The big deal now is Hy's." She shook her head. "No, meet me at The Keg on St. Mary Avenue. What time?"

"Eight o'clock?"

She considered. "Make it seven. I go to bed early."

They got up and moved to the cash register, where she let Salter pay for their lunch. As they stepped outside, a taxi pulled up and a couple got out. The man went into the motel office while the woman walked off to look at the highway.

"Can I ask you a question?" Adela asked.

Salter sighed. "Sure," he said.

"Are you married—still?"

"I told you I was."

"That's right. What would you do if you caught your wife having an affair?"

But Salter had seen the question coming. "It's not a question I have to worry about," he said.

"Really certain of yourself?"

"No. Really certain that I'd never catch her. And that's all of True Confessions for today."

"You're a coward."

"Right. And the older I get, the more difficult it is to

answer questions like that." He walked her to her car and looked around for a taxi for himself.

"You wanna go downtown?" a voice said. Salter looked down to see the cabbie's face leaning across the seat addressing him.

As they drove off, the cabbie said, "Nice work if you can get it," jerking his head at the woman now walking back to the motel office to meet her man, who was coming out.

Salter ignored him. For a few minutes he wanted to think about something other than adultery and jealousy and ethnic relations in Winnipeg.

Winnipeg's financial district is that area of downtown from which one can throw a stone through a window of the James Richardson building; McDermot Street, where Kowalczyk's company had its offices, is in the heart of the district.

Salter found Kowalczyk waiting for him. The engineer led him into a small room furnished with couches and a liquor cabinet where, Salter guessed, the company entertained its clients after a hard contract session. Around the walls were photographs of the plazas and malls the company had built.

Kowalczyk gave instructions to a little old lady in the front office and closed the door. He was a handsome man with a small acne scar on one cheek and black wavy hair. When his mouth was closed, his lips disappeared, giving his face a slightly embittered look. He was dressed in a well-cut, dark suit that looked as if it had been pressed an hour before. His hands were his most remarkable feature—giant, knobbly protuberances attached to very thin wrists. When they shook hands, Salter felt as if he was being grabbed by a mechanical clamp made of bones.

When they were seated, Salter led him through his movements on the weekend that his wife had been killed, and bumped into the problem that Kowalczyk had had enough time to have flown to Toronto and back, a lapse of time that was covered by his trip to close up his cottage, but not verified by any witnesses. Kowalczyk readily agreed that it was an awkward gap, and said, "That's your problem, Inspector. My lawyer says that if you had found anything else to connect me with Nancy's death you would have moved long ago."

It was true. Just for the exercise, Salter took him step by step through the rest of his story, but no detail changed.

"Did you tell your lawyer I was in town?"

"Yes, I did, as soon as my mother called me. He told me to cooperate with you completely. I told him I had nothing to do with Nancy's death and that I would like you people to find the killer."

"Why?"

"What do you mean, why?" Kowalczyk reacted forcefully as to a very stupid question. "She was my wife."

"But you were separated, about to get a divorce."

"She was still my wife."

"You had planned to fly to Toronto the following

weekend, according to your original statement. Why was that?"

"I told you people. To sort out the details of the divorce."

"Were you in touch with her on a regular basis?"

"No. She was going to get her own lawyer."

"What made you decide to get in touch with her now?"

Kowalczyk said, "It was time, that's all. What's the point of this?"

Salter said, "If she was in touch with you directly, or you with her, someone in Toronto might have been told, and told why, so I'm likely to come across it when I question everybody else."

"You know she wrote to me, don't you?"

"Yes, I do."

"I only got one letter from her, but she said she had tried to write to me several times. I think she must have written to the wrong address."

Salter let this pass as Kowalczyk's obvious defense of his mother. "But she got through to you eventually, didn't she?"

"Yes, through my office."

Salter made a mental note to assure Adela that he had got the story from Kowalczyk without involving her.

"And the letter asked you to come to Toronto about the divorce? That seem kind of strange?"

Kowalczyk took a small breath. "I just told that to your people to shut them up," he said. "It has nothing to do with you, but the truth was that we were going to get together to see if there was still any chance of making it again."

"Did you hope there was?"

"Yes, I did. Once."

"And did she?"

"I think so. I still have her letter. You want to see it?"

"Yes. Is it at home?"

"No." Kowalczyk reached into the inside pocket of his jacket for his wallet and fished out the letter from the lining. "Read it," he said.

Salter unfolded the single sheet of paper. "Dear Vic, I've written several times lately but not heard a thing from you so just in case you didn't get the letters I'm sending this care of your office. I can't go over all my letters again but they all say the same thing—could we get together and talk? I still have mostly good feelings about you and I wonder if we could talk about what happened and why it happened. My lawyer says that you have stopped moving on the divorce, so maybe you feel the same way. Why don't you come to Toronto for a weekend and maybe we can talk? I have a lot to say. Love (I mean it), Nancy."

Salter handed the letter back. "What was your response?"

"I called her and arranged to be in Toronto."

"You had hopes, did you? Why did you tell the police that the trip was arranged to wrap up the divorce?"

"Because it was private, not their business."

Salter said nothing, and Kowalczyk continued.

"When I got her letter I still thought there might be some possibility for us. And talking on the phone to her I got a bit carried away. As it happens, it wouldn't have made any difference. Your people told me what she had been doing."

"What?"

"The ad in the newspaper."

"That confirmed it for you, did it? That there was no hope?"

"What would *you* think? I had already caught her having an affair in Winnipeg."

"Do you know who with?"

"Yes, I do, but that's my business."

Salter looked around the room. "Do you have the keys to the liquor cabinet?" he asked. "I'd like a drink."

Kowalczyk looked slightly disconcerted. "Sure," he said. "I'm a partner. What do you want?"

"Beer, if you have any."

Kowalczyk opened a small refrigerator under the cabinet. "Labatt's?" he asked.

"That'll do." Salter waited until the beer was poured and started again. "First of all," he said, "the man may be a suspect. Anyone who had relations with your wife must be on our list, and this guy got missed in the original inquiry. So I have a new suspect. So I have to know his name. Maybe they were still having an affair."

"No. Nancy told me it was finished right then."

"And you believed her? She might have been lying."

"She never lied to me that I know of."

"Maybe he went to Toronto, looked her up, and tried to start it again."

"I thought of that. He was here in Winnipeg."

"You sure?"

"Yes. He told me."

"You mean you checked up on him yourself?"

"He was the only one I knew Nancy had ever been with. He works for a publisher in Toronto and he goes there a lot."

"You got into a fight with him once, didn't you?"

"Yes, but that's history, mister."

"What's his name? I have to know."

Kowalczyk said nothing for a few minutes. Then, "He'll know where you got his name. I have nothing against him now."

"No, he won't. I'll tell him we got an anonymous tip. This town is full of them. How's that?"

Kowalczyk smiled without any pleasure. Then, reluctantly, he got out his diary and gave Salter the name and address.

Salter pretended to consult a list of questions, checking them off. "Oh, yes," he said. "Did you ever go to Toronto to see your wife at any time since she moved away?"

"I never saw her after she left me," Kowalczyk said.

Salter put the list away and finished his beer. Without preamble, conversationally, he said, "What do you do with your canoe during the winter? Where do you store it?"

"Under the porch. I built a space for it when I added the porch."

Salter nodded. "It isn't there, Mr. Kowalczyk. We checked."

"When?" Kowalczyk asked. "When did you check?"

"Yesterday," Salter said. "We sent a man to have a look. There's no canoe there."

"Then someone stole it. I didn't think they would steal a canoe. Okay, I'll report it."

Well done, Orliff, Salter thought. He stood up.

"You think I could have killed Nancy?" Kowalczyk asked.

"I'm just eliminating people at this point," Salter said. He tried a small joke. "You don't have a private plane, do you?" he asked. "Or access to the company one?"

"No, I don't. This company isn't that big yet."

"I know. We checked that, too. Would you mind calling a cab for me?"

"Where are you staying?"

"The Marlborough."

"I'll drop you. It's on my way. My car is behind the building."

Salter put on his coat and looked around the room at the photographs of Kowalczyk's enterprises. "You're doing well," he said.

Kowalczyk closed the door of the liquor cupboard. "We're building two malls in Alberta and one in Saskatchewan," he said. "We're doing all right."

"And one in Ontario."

Kowalczyk looked surprised. Then he smiled. "You mean Raymond's Marketplace. No, that's just a toy. I've lent Raymond a little bit of money, but it's nothing to do with the company. We don't go in for things like that. But Raymond might make a go of it. I hope so."

They left through a back door and found Kowalczyk's car in a space with his name on it. On the way to the hotel, Salter put his last question. "Who else knew you were going to see your wife the following weekend?" he asked. "Your mother?"

Kowalczyk shook his head. "No, I didn't want to tell her until I had something to report. She didn't like Nancy," he confessed. "No, I didn't tell anyone except Adela."

The car drew up outside the hotel. As Salter was opening the door, Kowalczyk said, "Do you think you'll find the guy?"

Salter chose his reply carefully, just in case he could start a hare. "Oh, sure," he said. "We're nearly there."

Salter had plenty of time before he was due at the restaurant, and he spent some of it looking through his notes, wondering what else he could do before he left Winnipeg.

Nancy Cowell's life in Winnipeg had been routinely researched by the Winnipeg police. What emerged was what he expected: she had kept in touch with two friends from college with whom she had lunch occasionally; she and Victor had subscriptions to the local theater; she read a lot, and she was a good housewife.

In the last year she had broken out a little to take a part-time job at a local radio station. Salter thought of one or two more questions to ask Adela, enough to justify the dinner, and continued reading.

Kowalczyk himself had had a very successful career. He had begun by working for the same contractor his father had worked for. Why? Salter wondered. As a demonstration to his dead father that his son had made it out of the ditch? In a short time he had gone from engineering into real estate development and joined his present company, first as an employee, then as a junior partner, now as a senior with two other seniors. Like his father, he was trusted and hard-working. And, by all accounts, devoted to Nancy. There was no need to go over all this ground again.

Salter looked in the mirror and decided that Adela was worth another shave. He called Annie to confirm the absence of calamity at his house, kicked off his shoes, and lay down for a small nap.

An hour later he set off to get his dinner. The weather was seasonable: a howling wind blew along Portage Avenue, flinging dry, gritty snow in his face, which was already suffering from the twenty-below temperature, and after a couple of blocks he wished that he had taken a cab, but he had still some time to kill. He arrived at the restaurant shriveled inside his clothes and ordered a rye and ginger for old times' sake—he had not drunk rye since he was last in Winnipeg, but in those days everybody drank it, except the girls who drank rum and

Coke. One taste was enough to satisfy his nostalgia; he ordered a beer, and then Adela was standing at the table. He helped her off with her coat and she sat down and grabbed the menu.

"I want a shrimp cocktail with our special sauce, a sirloin steak with a baked potato with sour cream and chives, a chef's salad, and strawberry shortcake. Oh, and some celery and olives to start," she intoned.

Salter looked at the spare little figure under the round face in surprise and signaled the waiter.

She grabbed his arm. "I'm kidding," she said. "Isn't that what you used to have in the old days, though?" and she solemnly repeated her order, adding, "And Tia Maria afterward."

"So what do you really want?" Salter asked, recognizing the clowning as her way of getting over the initial awkwardness. "Yogurt and an apple?"

"Is that what you think I want? I'm an exercise fanatic, Mr.—" She broke off. "What do I call you?"

"Charlie will do."

"Right. I need my protein, Charlie. A small steak and a salad. And some wine, please." She sat back while he gave the order. When the waiter left, she said, "Okay. Start grilling me."

She'll relax in a minute, Salter thought. "A couple of things don't quite fit," he said. "In her ad, Nancy said she was interested in tennis and bridge, but one man I questioned said she couldn't play tennis. This guy may have had very high standards, but could she play? If she couldn't, why would she want to put that in the ad?"

The salad arrived, giving Adela time to think while she chewed her first mouthful. Then, "Tennis and bridge," she repeated. "No. She couldn't play tennis and she wasn't very good at bridge."

"Then why advertise that she wanted a guy who could?"

"Because that's the kind of man she wanted to respond. How can I explain? I tried to teach her tennis—I'm good, by the way—and after we'd been out three or four times she talked as if she were a tennis player. She liked the idea of being a tennis player—you know what I mean?" Adela ate some more salad. "She liked to try out new stuff. So when she took up bridge she did it for some other reason, like widening her interests, or some such, not because she was interested in bridge. It was the same with tennis. Am I making this clear? I'm not putting her down, but when she got into something, she did it with the idea of improving her life-style. Bridge improves your mind, tennis improves your body, and both will improve your social life, she thought. The same attitude went for her marriage. She practically took a course in marriage—'how to be a good wife.' She talked a lot about what a good wife was. And she became a professional Ukrainian."

"A what?"

"A Ukrainian. She married a Ukrainian, therefore the proper thing to do was to learn how to be a Ukrainian wife. She didn't quite convert to the Orthodox church, but damn near. She cooked Ukrainian food, read up on the history of the Ukraine—for a while I thought she was going to take up embroidery so she could make peasant blouses. Very heavy, and a bit embarrassing. She used to question me about our culture. What did I know? I'm a Canadian."

"You think that's why she advertised?"

"What?"

"From what you're saying she wasn't impulsive, and she wasn't advertising just because she needed a man . . ."

"Sex," she translated.

Salter nodded, and she jumped in. "Right," she said. "I never bothered to work it out, but it's the only way it makes sense. She got to Toronto, found she was lonely, asked herself what people in her position did, and came up with the answer—they advertise. A logical decision. She put in the tennis and bridge, not because she wanted to play, but because that's what she wanted to play *at*. Of course."

"But she did have an affair here."

"Sure," Adela said and rested her chin on her hands. Salter waited for more as he regarded the family resemblance that surfaced in her hands. Like her brother's, they were slightly too large and knobbly, the only unfeminine thing about her. Adela noticed his gaze and put her hands on her lap. "Another of Nancy's big decisions," she said.

The steak arrived and they ate in silence for a while.

"Would you have called her intelligent?" Salter asked.

Adela shook her head. "She got good grades and a master's degree, but she didn't have much savvy, no street smarts." She pushed her plate aside. "She was dumb to marry Victor." She sipped her wine. "He never deserved all this shit."

The dinner was over. Salter tried a new topic, but the life had gone out of the conversation, and he caught her looking at her watch. To break the silence, Adela put a question of her own, one, she said, that had occurred to her that afternoon. What, she asked, had been Salter's wife's reaction to the reappearance of his first wife after twenty-five years?

Salter considered the question. "It's not my first wife that bothers her," he said. "It's me. She's annoyed with me for having a first wife at all."

Adela laughed and stood up. While he paid the bill, she moved to a wall phone. Salter waited while she made three phone calls and realized he was not her whole evening, but an interlude. She had carved a small space in her day for him, and now his time was up. When she was finished with the phone, he offered to put her in a cab, but one of the phone calls had been to her boyfriend to pick her up. They waited by the door until he came, a handsome, ski-tanned character, dressed in a raccoon coat. They shook hands all around, and Adela and her friend drove off. Salter walked back down Portage, hustled along by the icy wind that was roaring in from the prairies. It had been better than eating alone, he thought. So what was it that was depressing him slightly? A raccoon coat?

The next morning Salter looked through the list of people who had known Nancy Cowell in Winnipeg and chose the name of a woman who had been in college with her. He called her number, identified himself, and explained that he was looking for witnesses who might have heard from her before her death. Then he read the names of the two passengers on the Friday flight to Toronto who had not been found.

"Do either of them ring a bell?" he asked.

"One of them sounds familiar," the woman said. "Read them again."

Salter did so.

"A. R. Harold," the woman repeated. "Tony Harold. He was at college with us. What's he up to now?"

"I don't know. Have you seen him lately?"

"Not for ten years. He lives in Moonee Ponds in Australia. Is he back? He would have called."

"Probably a coincidence," Salter said. "Thanks." He hung up.

He found John Kirby in his office, in a house on Macmillan Avenue. Kirby was the local representative of a Toronto publisher, and his office was also his basement. Kirby seemed impatient but quite ready to talk to him.

"What do you want to know?" Kirby began with a brisk air. "I had an affair with Nancy. No big deal. We met three times at the Pirate Inn on Tuesday afternoons. Somebody saw us, and the last time Vic was waiting for us when we came out."

"And jumped you?"

"Yeah. How'd you know that? A couple of guys moved in, and he turned around and drove off. The next day Nancy phoned to tell me that it was over with me and the next thing I heard she had moved to Toronto."

"And you never saw him or her again?"

"He came around a couple of weeks after she was killed. Once we started talking he wanted to stay around, and we spent the evening drinking and talking."

"About Nancy Cowell?"

"Sort of. It was kind of embarrassing until we had had enough to drink. But he was still in a bad state and I figured the least I could do was sit with him for a while."

"What did you talk about?"

Again Kirby looked embarrassed. "I told you—Nancy."

"What about her?" In a minute I'm going to ask you a nasty question, Salter decided.

Kirby waited a long time and then said, "He wanted to know what Nancy was like."

"In bed?" It came out, and Salter was ashamed, but it worked.

"For God's sake, Nancy was *dead.* He wanted to know what I knew about her. He was—he was jealous, you know?—but he was getting over it. He was going to visit her the week after she was killed, and now she was dead and all the old stuff came back."

"He had something to be jealous of, didn't he, with you around?"

"Look, buddy, I don't have to talk to you like this. We could go down to the station and I'll give you all the answers I'm supposed to. It'll take three minutes. But Vic phoned me last night. He said you seemed okay and that if I told you everything I knew, it might help. I don't know. You sound like a dink to me."

"Sorry. Kowalczyk is right. I'm just fishing around trying to pick up anything to give me a lead, like, for instance, how many guys Kowalczyk had to worry about."

"Okay, so keep it clean, eh? Nancy was Victor's whole world, but by the time I came along he had already screwed it up. I didn't have anything to do with it. When he came around he was beginning to see that, so I let him talk about it."

"How did he screw it up?"

"By being jealous all the time. I was probably the only guy Nancy ever went with, and by then their marriage was finished."

"What about before she was married?"

"She didn't screw around. She came with me because she had had enough of being a good wife and getting no credit for it. She wasn't a nun. You know that when she and I started meeting she hadn't slept with Vic for six months? I know that because of the way she was with me."

"You mean frustrated, repressed?"

"No, for God's sake. What's the matter with you? I mean she was scared all the time, guilty as hell, and only doing it with me because of the way he was treating her." Kirby glanced at the door and lowered his voice. "I've had a lot of relationships! I never figured to get married, but I'd like some kids, and I'm telling you Nancy was no floozie."

"But she fell in love with you? How did you meet?"

"No. I was just handy when she decided to hell with it. She worked part time at a radio station doing book reviews and I used to wheel visiting authors in to see her. She wasn't in love with anyone except Vic. We wouldn't have lasted long because she was too much trouble—wouldn't come to my apartment, wouldn't let me phone her at work. Very complicated."

"I thought she was a social worker."

"She was. But Vic didn't want her to work, so she stayed home for years. Then she got this part-time job doing interviews and reviews."

Kirby was relaxed again and Salter put the question once more. "What did Kowalczyk want to know?"

"He was like you. He wanted to know if Nancy was promiscuous, and I told him no. I told him how wrong he had been about her. Maybe I should have let it alone, but it didn't seem fair to Nancy, and besides, he seemed to feel better afterward. I don't know, though. Probably when he woke up next morning he didn't believe me. He's a case, that one. I like the guy, but I can see he would drive any woman crazy."

"Who was doing all the damage?"

"I think he was doing it to himself."

"But someone saw you at the motel and called him."

"That could have been anyone. I told Nancy that if we were seen it would be a lot more obvious than if she were seen leaving my place, and there was a lot more chance of it. This is Winnipeg, you know, the Athens of the Tundra, but it's just a small town, really."

"Do you know anyone who had it in for him?"

"Or for her? No. I didn't know the guy that well. I do know that he was very proud of Nancy and someone might have wanted to take him down a peg."

"Do you know his sister?"

"Adela?" Kirby queried. Then, "Yeah, I know her."

"How well?"

"What's that got to do with anything?" Kirby challenged. "We've been friends for years. Why?"

Salter backed off. He had been intending to ask Kirby something about the relationship between Adela and her brother, but he had stumbled into a sensitive area. "I just wondered if she was the one to ask about Nancy, but I'll ask her anyway," Salter extemporized, adding quickly, "You travel to Toronto occasionally, don't you?"

"Sure. I used to split my time between here and Toronto, but I'm here full time now."

"Did you ever see Nancy when you went to Toronto?"

"Yes, a couple of times when she first went East."

Salter waited.

"We didn't continue the relationship, if that's what you're getting at."

Salter waited some more.

"The night Nancy got killed I was here in Winnipeg," Kirby said. He glanced over his shoulder. "As a matter of fact I was up at Clear Lake that weekend."

"Where's that?"

"In the National Park."

"On your own?"

"No." Kirby looked over his shoulder again. "With a girl."

"Could she confirm that?"

"If we had to. Do we?" Once more Kirby was on the edge of a challenge.

"Did you stay at a motel?"

"Yeah. But I didn't use my own name."

"Why not? Who cares nowadays?"

"I got nailed once. I was with someone, and her husband was having her watched. This private detective found out who she was registered with and reported back to her husband."

"So?"

"Her husband knew me."

"So now you're more careful. I see."

"So now I'm getting married soon. I told you."

"Can I check with the girl you were with?"

"Am I a suspect or something? No, you can't."

"Why? Is she married?"

Kirby stayed silent. "All right," Salter said. "Maybe

when you think about it you might want to think of some way we could check it. Just in case I'm asked." He looked around as the door opened. A girl about fifteen years younger than Kirby stood in the doorway.

"Are you and Mr. Salter staying for lunch?" she asked. She seemed shy of interrupting them but eager to be a proper hostess for Kirby.

She doesn't know I'm a cop, thought Salter. Kirby looked away and Salter took the hint. "No thanks," he said. "I have to be on the afternoon plane back to Toronto."

Kirby jumped up and put out his hand. "You're welcome," he said, and hustled Salter out into the street.

Salter had learned something from the horse's mouth about Nancy Cowell and the difficult relationship she had had with her husband. Something else, too. He thought he had learned that Kirby had once had an affair with Adela, which had nothing to do with his case, but confirmed Kirby as an authority on the Kowalczyks. He walked along Macmillan to Stafford, where he hoped to flag a cab. When one finally appeared he had learned why Winnipeg policemen used to wear coats made of buffalo hide.

He had just finished packing his bag when the telephone rang. It was Adela Cowell. She began without any preliminaries.

"I've been speaking with John Kirby," she said. "You want to know who he was with at Clear Lake, don't you? Well, he was with me, so you can cross him off your list. Okay?"

"Why didn't he say so?" Salter asked.

"Why the hell do you *think*? Because he was afraid you'd blab it to Vic, for one thing, and he thought I might not want Vic to know. And for another thing, John's fiancée was in the next room. Is that enough? Now leave him alone."

"Did you have a good time?" Salter asked mildly.

"*What*?"

"Was the weather nice?"

"What the hell is that supposed to mean? Yes, it was. John and I went skinny-dipping at midnight. Under a full moon. Is that what you wanted to know?"

"I just wondered," Salter said. "Thanks for the call."

She hung up in his ear.

Salter turned back to the notes of his original conversation with Mrs. Cowell, Adela's mother, and found the reference he was looking for. Adela had spent the weekend with relatives in Dauphin, according to her mother, relatives that the old lady probably called twice a week to chat with. "Oh, you stupid, stupid woman," he said to himself as he put the notebook away. "Don't you know this is homicide?" So far, though, it was just a lie, and he was a long way from knowing what it meant.

Chapter

7

"I had lunch with Gerry today," Annie said after supper.

"Who?"

"Gerry, your first wife."

Salter took this in. "And who suggested that?" he asked.

"She did. She called me at home last night. I guess she found out that you were out of town, and it looked like a chance to get together."

"What happened? Did you let your hair down?" Salter spoke in a jocular tone, but he really wanted to know. Why were they having lunch? What was Gerry up to? Most of all, what did they talk about?

"What did you talk about?" he asked.

"You."

"That must have been fascinating."

"It was interesting."

I'll bet. "What was?"

"Relax, Charlie. She just wanted to get a look at me, and I was curious too. But I don't want her around, thanks."

Salter relaxed slightly. "She lives in another world," he said. "I thought she'd gone to pieces a bit, though not so much as some of them, I guess."

"Some of who?"

"The women's-movement crowd."

"What do you mean, gone to pieces?"

"She doesn't do anything to herself. Look at her clothes and stuff."

"What about them?"

"She doesn't care what she looks like."

"She seemed quite clean and tidy."

"Who wants that—clean and tidy?"

"Next time you meet her, take a good look. I think she's stopped putting on warpaint, that's all."

"What do you mean? Makeup? I noticed that."

"It's more than makeup. She just doesn't dress for men anymore. She doesn't care what she looks like as long as she is comfortable when she passes a mirror. She dresses to suit herself, like a lot of men."

"Has she given up men, then?"

"Maybe, but not necessarily. *I've* reached the age or the stage where I don't care what men look like, as long as they're interesting. She has, too. I think that she's only interested in men who are interested in her, not in her looks. I wish I didn't care. About myself, I mean."

"I'm glad you do. I'm not ready for you in army boots."

"I know."

"What do you think she wants, then? To find a man who'll appreciate her?"

"I told you. I don't think she cares about that. I suspect that a lot of men find her attractive—no, that's not the word—want to be with her. To tell you the truth, I think she has become religious."

"She's never been near a church in her life, except to marry me."

"That's not what I meant. But it's the only way I can describe it. She seemed like someone on her way to becoming a nun. She's not interested in herself, or not much. I think you'll find her camping out on that common in England one of these days. Something like that."

"The antinuclear crowd?"

"Yes. She told me she thinks it's all hopeless, that the end of the world is coming, but if there's a chance she wants to do what she can."

"But she's got a kid. A sixteen-year-old. Did she tell you he wants to join the Mounties? They'll be on opposite sides of the barricades."

"Yes, we had a little chuckle about that. But she'll look after him for another couple of years, until he goes off to the Yukon, and then she's free. You were right about him, by the way; she says he doesn't approve of her."

"Will you see her again?"

"No, I told you. I'm hung up on my own life. I'm glad I met her, though. I had no idea from you what she was like and I wondered why you married her. Now I know."

"Tell me."

"Because she's rare, Charlie. Even if you don't see it anymore, you must have once. She must have made you feel very special."

"Could we talk about Christmas?" Salter asked. He wanted time to digest this conversation, to absorb it properly.

"Sure," Annie said promptly. "I talked your dad around. He's coming, but he wants to take us all out to dinner on Christmas Eve. So that he won't be at a disadvantage on Boxing Day, I guess."

"Where? Ed's Warehouse?" Salter laughed.

"That's right, and I've told Mother and Dad, and they are happy about it. Now all I have to worry about is Christmas Day."

"I'll look forward to seeing your mother in a straw boater," Salter said.

"Only the waiters wear straw hats. And if your father wants to take us out for dinner then my parents can make the effort to enjoy it."

"God bless us, every one," Salter said. The remark triggered an objection. "We'll miss the movie," he said. On Christmas Eve for the last ten years the Salters had watched *A Christmas Carol* on television. It was a pleasure that Salter and Annie had long tired of, but now that Seth was beginning to learn it by heart too, they would probably have to watch it for another three or four years.

"No, we won't. It comes on twice, and we can watch it after everyone has gone home."

"Where are we going on Boxing Day?"

"Dad won't tell me. It's a surprise."

"Not too much of one, I hope. He knows that my dad doesn't have a tux, doesn't he?"

"He knows. It'll be somewhere nice. Let it happen. Did you get Angus's jacket yet?"

"I'm making inquiries. Don't nag."

"There're only fifteen more shopping days left."

"They're taking bets on you in Homicide," Wycke said. "Or rather Marinelli is laying odds against you. He can't find any takers."

The two men were sitting by the window of an English-type bar miraculously contained within an office building on the corner of College and Yonge.

"What odds is he giving?" Salter asked. "I might take him on."

"You on to something?"

Salter said, "If word got around that I was betting on myself, the odds would come down and you could get in on the other side."

Wycke laughed. "Nothing, eh?"

"Not nothing. I've eliminated the possibility that she was killed by a one-night stand."

"That's something, isn't it? Eliminates about a million guys in Toronto."

"But there's still the strong likelihood that some drifter managed to get in, a weirdo."

"That narrows it down to about five thousand."

"Then there's a third man we haven't found yet."

Wycke laughed. "Who is the Third Man?" he asked.

Salter ignored Wycke's facetiousness. "She went out with three guys that we know of. Two of them we've checked out, but I haven't found the third yet; Gatenby will probably pick him up this afternoon. Did I tell you how Gatenby found him?" He recounted his sergeant's device, glad of the chance to divert Wycke's questions.

"Genius," Wycke said admiringly.

"But I'm not getting my hopes up. Even if this guy was with her that evening, he probably didn't kill her."

"Then why hasn't he come forward?"

There was no need to answer Wycke's question.

"The trouble is, Charlie, the public just doesn't trust us," Wycke said, adopting a tone of mock sincerity.

The two men sat and watched the snow falling past the window. "Christmas all wrapped up?" Wycke asked.

"Just about. I still haven't found the little white outdoor lights I told you about."

"Try Canadian Tire."

"I tried them."

"Try Eaton's, Simpson's. Maybe Aikenheads'."

"Harry, I tried all those. Have you actually seen them on sale anywhere?"

Wycke considered. "No," he said.

"Nor have I. If you do, let me know."

"Did you try New York? I've seen them there."

"You know anyone who is flying down to New York in the next ten days who would spend an afternoon looking for Christmas lights for me?"

"Not offhand."

"If you do, let me know."

"Sounds to me as if you've got yourself into one of those things where you know that what you want is *somewhere* and you trudge your ass off for two weeks trying to find it. I did that one year. Alice wanted one of those butter dishes that you stand in water and it keeps the butter cool in summer. You know the kind I mean?"

"Uh-huh," Salter said, who didn't, but the end of the story was obvious enough.

"Somebody brought her back one from England, and she broke it, so I tried to find her another one. Just a stocking thing, you know. I went everywhere looking for one. Even out to Oakville where there's a store that sells old country stuff. They had them, they said, last year, but they were sold out. I never did find one. Nearly spoiled my Christmas. Give up, buddy. Or get one of the rounders to steal you a set from outside a boutique in Yorkville."

"I may do that. Now I've got to go. Annie's working late tonight and I have to get supper."

"Hamburger Helper?"

"No. The boys are meeting me in Fran's."

"Don't forget to take it out of the housekeeping money. Make these women pay for their liberation."

Later, over cheeseburgers and hot chocolate, Salter confided his problem with the Christmas lights to the two boys and got them interested. They agreed to give it a week, during which time they would check every hardware store they passed.

The next morning Gatenby led in a very frightened man, Atterbury, the insurance agent.

"Let's get to the point, Mr. Atterbury. We are checking all known contacts of Nancy Cowell, who was found murdered in her apartment a while ago. Our investigation has uncovered the possibility that you knew her."

Atterbury shook his head violently. "I only met her once, sir," he said. "Just once. I answered her ad and we had some drinks. That's all."

"When?"

"About a month before she was killed."

"You knew she'd been murdered, did you?"

"Sure, it was in all the papers." Atterbury was in an agony of apprehension.

"Where were you when she died?"

"At home," Atterbury burst out. "At home."

Jesus Christ, another one, thought Salter. "Watching television?" he asked.

"No. We were playing bridge with some neighbors."

"We?"

"My wife and me."

Salter looked at the man, feeling pity fighting a losing

battle with other, more negative emotions. "How do I confirm this?" he asked.

"I don't know, except by asking my wife. She has it marked on the kitchen calendar."

"Would you like us to make up a story?" Salter asked.

Atterbury looked at the end of his rope. "Could you?" he asked. "Could you maybe check the whole street or something?"

It was probably enough. "What are your neighbors' names?" Salter asked. "On both sides, for a few houses down."

But Atterbury was in no condition to remember anything.

"Come back this afternoon, with a list," Salter said, and turned away as Atterbury scrambled out of the office.

When he had gone, Salter looked at Gatenby quizzically. By some kind of consent, neither man said anything until Salter found the next step. "She had dinner with someone," he said. "But all these guys claimed they stayed home."

"We could check to see if they ate out somewhere," Gatenby said. "Everybody charges meals these days. I'll call Visa and Mastercard and find out if any of them had a meal on his account that night."

"That's right," Salter said. "She had a hundred dollars in her purse, so the chances are that she didn't pay for the dinner. You're getting better and better, Frank. Wait. While you're at it, find out if any of these people charged anything by credit card on Friday or Saturday.

And check up on a guy named A. R. Harold of Moonee Ponds, in Australia. Find out where he was that weekend."

Gatenby looked at the list. "Her too?" he asked.

"Her too," Salter said. "Find out about them all." Salter brooded over what he had learned in Winnipeg and considered driving out to talk to Tranby about it. But winter had now arrived in Toronto, and the prospect of tramping around Mitcham Marketplace in the snow was enough to put him off. He went back to his solitary brooding.

An hour later a mildly excited Gatenby had got as far as the second name on his list.

"Atterbury never charged anything that night," he said. "But this guy did." Henning, the journalist, had charged a dinner that night at Movenpick, a Swiss restaurant downtown.

Salter picked up Henning's statement.

"He's lying, isn't he?" Gatenby continued. "But he was at work when she was killed, so what's his problem? Another Atterbury?"

"No. I'll tell you. We'll have to break down his supervisor. Henning has a perfect alibi—that's always suspicious. What happened was this: Henning killed Nancy Cowell and then went off to work. The time was now eleven-forty-five."

"But . . ."

"Hold on. When he got to work, he found his supervisor passed out at his desk. Drunk. You know what these hard-drinking front-page guys are like. Henning realized that he had a perfect setup. The supervisor doesn't wear a watch, see. *Real* old-time journalists think wristwatches are faggy. So all Henning had to do was move the office clock back an hour, wake up his boss, point out the time, and then get his boss into a cab and send him home. All the boss remembers is that Henning turned up on time. He couldn't confess to us that he was hammered. The perfect crime."

Gatenby laughed with glee. "That's it," he cried. "But he forgot to change the clock back, so when we check the next shift we find someone who remembers that the clock was an hour slow the next morning. They always make a mistake, don't they? Henning had no idea he would come up against us."

"Poor bastard," Salter said. "Better get him in here, so we can hit him with it."

"There's just one problem. There are five other guys in Henning's office. What were they doing when Henning was standing on the ladder changing the clock?"

"They were all *young* guys," Salter said. "Stoned out of their minds on mescaline or whatever they're into these days. Just in case we're wrong, though, keep checking the others. And let's find out why Henning was lying to us. He may solve a problem I'm having."

Salter called the press agency, established that Henning's shift was finished at three-thirty, and told him to come in to the station before he went home.

At first Henning bluffed. "Okay," he said in his Slim Pickens voice. "So I was out to dinner that night. But not with Nancy. Not with Nancy, I'll tell you. In fact," he leaned forward, "I can't tell you who I was with that night. I can tell you her name, but I sure as hell don't know where you could find her. I've tried. I met her through an ad, like I did with Nancy. I answered four or five of them that weekend."

"Give me her name, we'll find her. Or don't you remember?"

"Betty. Betty Smith."

"What was she like?"

"Kinda medium size, fair hair. Pretty little gal."

"Where did you go afterward?"

"We went for a ride around."

"Then you took her home?"

"No. She wouldn't let me see where she lived. Like Nancy."

"Did you see her again?"

"No. I guess I wasn't smart enough for her." As he entered his own fiction, Henning began to elaborate. "I figured she was looking for a snappier-type guy, you know? She was dressed for dancing herself."

"And you don't have her phone number."

"That's right. Never did have."

"We'll find her," Salter said. He exuded a phony calm. "Okay, Mr. Henning, and if Miss Smith confirms your story I won't bother you again. Thanks for coming in."

"How are you going to locate her?"

"Was her ad in the same day as Nancy Cowell's?"

"The exact same day, Inspector."

"My sergeant will find her. I don't know how he does it, but we'll locate her by tomorrow morning, if she exists. Thanks, Mr. Henning."

Henning reappeared the next morning, but not before a call from Wycke had alerted Salter. "Louis Tannenbaum is representing one of your suspects," Wycke said. "Guy named Henning. He's coming in to see you this morning."

Tannenbaum. One of Toronto's top criminal lawyers.

"What did you tell him?"

"I didn't tell him anything, but he's found out from somewhere, probably one of my people, that Cowell was murdered in the small hours, which lets his client off the hook, he says."

"Pity. Okay. It doesn't matter. I was just tidying up a detail while I was checking some other stuff."

Tannenbaum and Henning were announced shortly after that, and Tannenbaum came right to the point. "Leave us alone for a minute, Mr. Henning, will you? I need a word with the inspector."

Henning went back out to the corridor and Tannenbaum closed the door after him. Then he sat down and smiled at Salter after checking his watch.

"Nice work," he said. "You got my client scared shitless. You know he didn't do it, so what's the name of the game?"

"He's lied to us. I think he was out with Nancy Cowell the night she was murdered. He may have been the last to see her, except the killer. I don't think he killed her, but what's he lying for?"

"Why do you *think,* Inspector? Last summer he reads —no, he writes, for Chrissake, he *writes* a story about a guy who was arrested for rape. Positive identification. A week before his trial the real rape artist is found. You guys knew that the guy you were charging wasn't guilty, but you were going to send him up anyway. There's a sergeant quoted in the story, 'We all knew he didn't do it, and we were working against time trying to find the real villain before this guy had to go to trial.' "

"We had a positive identification. What did you expect us to do?"

"Yeah, well. I mean, Christ, what does the public think? *I* know you had to go ahead, but Henning remembers this and thinks you'll do the same to him. Fortunately someone put him on to me, and my connections told me the thing that you hadn't told Henning, namely, that this woman was killed when my client was at work, had been for an hour at least. So what are you trying to do?"

"Find the real killer like we did last time."

"Okay, so let's take my boy off the hook, shall we?"

"Tell Henning to come in," Salter said.

Tannenbaum went to the door and jerked his head at Henning, who came in and sat down.

The lawyer spoke. "Okay. Let's all start again. This is very informal, Mr. Henning. No one is taking notes. No one is warning you. Right, Inspector?"

Salter ignored the lawyer. "Mr. Henning," he said.

"Nancy Cowell was killed while you were at work, and we do not regard you as a suspect. I told you that yesterday."

"You didn't tell me why, though."

"I wouldn't be telling you now if your lawyer didn't have a wire into our files. So now you know. I'd still like to know what you were doing that evening. So far you have said you were watching television, then you said that you were having dinner with someone called Betty Smith." Here Salter looked at Tannenbaum, who threw up his hands in a gesture of despair and looked at his watch. Salter continued. "We've checked that out now. No one called Betty Smith placed an ad that day. Maybe she gave you a false name? Can you tell us anything more about her?"

"How long do you plan to question my client?" Tannenbaum interrupted. "I have to appear before the Court of Appeals at ten o'clock."

"I don't give a fuck what you have to do, Mr. Tannenbaum. Mr. Henning might be able to help us and as long as you don't make a legal objection, I'd like to see if he knows anything that might be helpful."

Tannenbaum looked at Salter, then at Henning, who looked back at Tannenbaum for guidance. Salter waited. Then Tannenbaum sighed and turned to face his client. Before he could speak, Salter cut in. "You want a few minutes alone?" he asked.

"No," Tannenbaum said. He addressed himself again to Henning. "Tell the policeman what he wants to know and let's get out of here."

Henning said, looking at his feet, "I took Nancy Cowell out to dinner that night."

"Thank you, Mr. Henning. Perhaps your lawyer will tell you why it was important that we know that."

"If you were with her," Tannenbaum explained, "then some other guy came along afterward. If they don't know about you, then they're looking for someone who was with her all the time, see?"

"Thank you," Salter said. "Okay, Mr. Henning. What time did you take her home?"

"About nine-thirty."

"What time did you leave her?"

"Around ten-thirty. I was a bit late for work."

"Did you have sex with her?"

"Hell, no. We just talked."

"Did she tell you anything about anyone else in her life? Mr. Tannenbaum could explain, but let me. If you spent three or four hours with her—by the way, how many times did you take her out? You told me just three before."

"I guess it was a bit more than that. Maybe half a dozen times."

"You got along well with her, didn't you?"

"Yeah. She was real nice."

"So can you remember anything? Did she discuss her husband at all?"

Tannenbaum cut in. "We're on the level now, eh, Salter? You're just looking for help, right? My client is not suspected of anything?"

"Right, Mr.—" Salter looked at a slip of paper on his

desk, a note from Gatenby about what he owed for the coffee fund—"Tannenbaum," he said. "Right. Your client has lied to us and thus made my job more difficult —obstructed us, in my opinion, though I'm not a lawyer. Now we're just talking, enlisting the aid of the public."

"Good. I'll leave you to it." He turned to Henning. "Cooperate," he said. "Don't worry. You won't get in the papers. Will he?" he asked Salter.

"Not unless we charge him with obstructing."

"So cooperate," Tannenbaum said. "Give me a call this afternoon." He nodded to Salter and left.

"Anything else?" Salter asked when the door closed.

Henning shook his head. "She wouldn't talk about her husband," he said. "But she was expecting him in town the next weekend. Did you know that?"

"That's what I want to hear," Salter said, as if it was news to him. "Anything else? Did she seem worried or excited by the prospect?"

"Not that I could tell. She only told me because I asked her for a date that weekend."

"Did you get the impression that she expected her husband to stay with her?"

"I don't know. But she was setting aside all her time for him."

"What about anyone else? Did she talk about any other friends?"

"She was going to the St. Lawrence Market the next day, that's all."

"Okay. Talk to your lawyer this afternoon and tell

him what you told us. I'll call you if I need you again." Salter nodded to the man, and he left.

"Kowalczyk's story still has a hole in it, doesn't it?" Wycke asked. They were eating hamburgers in Toby's on Bloor Street. The quality of the hamburgers, according to Wycke, just made up for the noise.

"I guess," Salter said.

"What are you going to do now?" Wycke asked.

"Wait for something to break."

"How do you mean? Break which way?"

But Salter could not explain himself, and had no intention of trying. "If I don't get anything else," he said, "I'll give it back to you. Soon."

"What are you up to, Charlie?"

"Me?" Salter asked. "Me? I'm looking for a killer. Remember?"

The afternoon passed peacefully enough. At the office there was a message for him to phone home immediately, most urgent, but when he called it was Seth to say he hadn't found any white lights but there were these terrific colored lights at the local hardware store and should he get them. Salter thanked the boy solemnly and said he would still like white ones if he could get them, and to keep looking. Then, to fill in time, he went through the Yellow Pages, letting his fingers do the walking. He phoned every Christmas-light manufacturer in Metro and got one positive response, that one company used to manufacture the lights he wanted but they no longer did so, and his best hope was to find a store that still had some old stock. Gatenby, who was in and out of his office while he was on the phone, acquainted himself with the problem and promised to join the hunt. "Don't worry about it, Frank," Salter said. "Just if you happen to see them." There was a dimension of the ridiculous about his quest if it should ever get around the station.

Once embarked, he set about purchasing a sheepskin jacket for Angus. This time he employed cunning, and phoned home again and spoke to Angus. He explained his predicament to the boy: Gatenby, his sergeant, he said, had a nephew who wanted a sheepskin jacket, and Gatenby had asked him (Salter) to get Angus's advice. What was a sheepskin jacket? Where were they to be found? What was the best kind? How much did they cost? What size was Angus, who, Gatenby figured, was about his nephew's size, maybe a shade smaller? Angus had all this information at his fingertips, and concluded, "Lucky sonofagun. I'd like one of those jackets."

"No way, son," Salter said. "We've already bought your present. Save up your Christmas money and buy one yourself. They'll probably be on sale after Christmas." Then he called Gerry to report progress.

"Okay, Charlie," she said. "I can see you're doing your best."

"I hear you and Annie had a nice time together," he said.

"Yes, we got along well. She doesn't live in my world,

and I couldn't live in hers, but I can see why you married her. She's what you always wanted. You're very lucky."

"She said that about you."

"What?"

"She could see why I married you."

Gerry laughed. "Looking forward to Christmas?" she asked.

This gave Salter an opportunity to give her a rundown on the various successes he had had to date, his failure to find white lights, and his fear of the possible frictions that the mix of relatives would create.

"It sounds nice," she said.

Although there was no emotion in her voice, no sadness, no longing, no yearning, just the sound of someone pleased for him, Salter was stricken with an impulse to share the good things with her. "You staying home?" he asked. "With the boy?"

"Yes."

That's where her life-style breaks down, he thought. At times like Christmas it must be lonely outside the normal world of family and friends. "You could join us if you like," he suggested, brushing aside the need to consult again with Annie.

"Well, thanks, but I've already made arrangements," she said with some hesitation.

"But won't it be quiet?" he asked, meaning lonely.

"I'm cooking dinner for seventeen people," she said. "On Christmas Eve some Jamaican friends are having everyone over. On Boxing Day we're all going up to a farm for cross-country skiing, about thirty of us. I'm quite looking forward to it."

"I see," Salter said. "I'll talk to you later." He hung up.

Then, as he was fiddling with a draft of his report, his telephone rang again. "Call for you from Kenora," the operator said.

"Melnyk here," another voice said. "O.P.P. Kenora. We found your canoe."

"You what?"

"There was a report put in a little while ago by a man named Kowalczyk, listing a stolen canoe. We found it but the police in Winnipeg told me you were interested and to tell your first."

"Yes? Well?"

"We know who stole it. We have him here."

"Good. What's this got to do with us?" Salter asked. His mind had long been working in other channels.

"We think he may have important information bearing on your case."

"Like what?"

"He can confirm that Kowalczyk was at his cottage on the Saturday and the Sunday."

"He can *what*?" Salter asked, remembering.

"He observed him on both days."

"Jesus Christ. Is he there? Let me talk to him."

A voice, hopeless, mournful, came on the line. "Yessir?"

"You saw Mr. Kowalczyk on the Saturday and Sunday, at his cabin?"

"Yessir."

"All right, what was he doing?"

"On Saturday he spent all day fishing, and on Sunday he closed up the cabin and left."

"What time in the morning did you first see him on Saturday?"

"First thing. Right after breakfast. We seen him Friday night, too."

"Friday night? You sure it was him?"

"Sure, sitting on his porch when we first went to have a look. Clear as daylight, it was."

"Why were you watching him?"

"We was hoping to see what he had left."

"You were checking his cabin out, to steal stuff?"

"Yessir. We didn't think he would be around."

"How do you know it was him? Do you know him?"

"Yessir. I repaired his dock last summer."

"And now you were going to steal his canoe."

"He used to leave it under his porch. Some of the Indians would have got it if we didn't."

"All right. Put me back to the officer."

When Melnyk came on the line Salter asked him what they knew about the man, and whether he could be trusted, though why anyone would confess unless he had done it was not obvious.

"It's him all right," the officer said. "There's been a lot of thefts this fall on the river, and we were watching this guy. When we turned his shack over, in October, we found a whole bunch of stuff that had been reported missing. He also took a couple of coats from Kowalczyk's place."

"How come this hasn't turned up before? You found this canoe in October, you say?"

"It didn't have any identification that we could trace, and the coats could've been anybody's. He said it was all his, until I pulled him in today. He's already served his time for the other stuff. Now we'll charge him with this."

"Can you identify the canoe positively now?"

"Sure. When Kowalczyk reported it missing, he told us where to find the I.D. number under the metal stripping. We knew the canoe was probably stolen and we'd held it here until we could find someone who could identify it. When the report came in, one of our guys remembered it."

"Okay. Thanks." Salter put the phone down and stared out at the frozen street for a while, wondering why he felt so good. Because he wasn't in Homicide, he decided.

And because, at last, the message had got through to him. He sat still, recalling all the conversations he had had about that fatal weekend, the conversation with Tranby, the truth surrounding the lie that Adela Cowell had told him, and especially the conversation with Gerry about what she had learned from Adela Cowell's friends.

"There goes our best suspect," Gatenby said.

"No, Frank. Now I know who did it, I think. But a couple of details first. Let's get that journalist, Henning, in here. No, better yet, what's his lawyer's number?"

A few minutes later Salter had talked to Tannenbaum and told him exactly what he wanted to know, and why. Then he waited. Tannenbaum called back in ten minutes and promised to be in Salter's office in half an hour.

When Tannenbaum and Henning arrived, Gatenby placed chairs for them, and Tannenbaum nodded to Henning to speak.

Henning said, "I did have sex with her."

Salter looked at Tannenbaum, who shrugged.

"I see," Salter said. "We are changing our story again, are we?"

"My client didn't understand your question before," Tannenbaum said.

"Let's have it then, Mr. Henning. You did have sex with Nancy Cowell. When? Between nine-thirty and eleven?"

"Yes."

"Why didn't you say so?"

"I don't know. I figured you would catch me on it in some way."

"Why are you telling me now?"

"Mr. Tannanbaum told me to." Henning looked very frightened.

"He thought it might be illegal, Inspector. The girl was raped, he heard, and maybe there's some kind of technical rape he didn't know about." Tannenbaum looked at Salter with his eyebrows raised. These civilians, the look said.

Salter acknowledged the look. "Did you rape her, Mr. Henning? Force her to have sex against her wish?"

"Hell, no, it wasn't like that. She was very willing," Henning whined.

"Tell him what it *was* like," Tannenbaum said in some disgust.

"Well, we'd been going out a few times, y'see, and I figured tonight was the night and I was kinda lookin' forward to it. I paid for the dinner, too, and I figured that meant something. We'd spent a lot of time together and I figured it ought to go somewhere, you know what I mean?"

"And she agreed."

"Not right away." Henning looked at his lawyer.

"Tell him, for Christ's sake," Tannenbaum said. "This is the part that might help."

"She said no at first, while we were having dinner. Her husband was coming the next weekend and she wasn't going to see me anymore. She wouldn't have come that night, but she couldn't get hold of me to cancel. But I talked her around, and we went back to her place."

"You talked her around?" Salter asked.

"She took pity on him, for God's sake," the lawyer said.

"That right, Mr. Henning?"

Henning wriggled in his chair. "She said okay, she didn't want to be unfair, but it would have to be the first and last time, because she couldn't see me anymore. She kind of joked about it. I didn't force her or anything."

"What did she say, do you remember?"

"Yeah. She called it our farewell debut."

Salter avoided Tannenbaum's eye. "In view of what you are now saying, Mr. Henning, can you tell us anymore about how she was looking forward to her husband's visit?"

"She was really looking forward to it. Not too much interest in me or anything else."

"Okay. A few details. Where did you make love? On the couch?"

"No. We got into bed."

"And when you left her, was she still in bed?"

"No. She put her nightgown and some kind of wrap on, and we had a little talk before I left."

"Okay. That checks. Goodbye, Mr. Henning."

Tannenbaum was already out the door, and Henning started to follow. Salter called him back. "One thing, Mr. Henning. The next time you hire an expensive lawyer like Tannenbaum, take his advice. It's cheaper in the end. It's like a dentist. This way you have to pay for two visits."

"Got him?" Gatenby asked, when the door closed.

"Nearly," Salter said. "What did you hear from Moonee Ponds?"

"I spoke to A.R. Harold's wife. She said he hadn't been out of Australia for ten years."

"Good," Salter said. "Next another word with my ex-wife. What else have we got to do? Yes, right. Frank, you're the credit-card wizard. Find out if this person withdrew any money from a banking machine on that Friday or Saturday, will you? No, let's be methodical. Find out if any of these three did."

"No way," Gatenby said. "I was lucky to get by the credit-card companies, because we're supposed to have a warrant. The Privacy Act."

"Shit. We won't get a warrant for all three. They'll call it a fishing expedition. Okay. I'm sure I'm right. I'll see Orliff and get a warrant for this one. I'll call you from City Hall." He telephoned ahead and got Gerry to meet him in the cafeteria. "Bring those notes you made," he requested.

She was waiting for him with coffee ready. "Getting somewhere?" she asked.

"Yes, but I'm not saying a word. I'm superstitious. Now, tell me exactly what you learned from those women."

She began her summary again. He stopped her three times, whenever she was quoting Nancy Cowell as reported by her friends. When she was finished, he got up to go.

"Hey," Gerry said. "When do I get to know what's going on?"

"Soon," Salter promised. He went out into the rotunda and called Gatenby.

"Adela Cowell phoned from Winnipeg," Gatenby said. "She wants you to call her."

"And the warrant?"

"It's promised," Gatenby said.

"Okay. I'll come back and make that call to Winnipeg. Then there are just two more details. One of them will have to wait until we get that warrant."

He returned to his office and got through to Adela Cowell immediately. She had obviously been sitting by the phone.

"I've been thinking," she said, in a tight, hard voice.

"Yes?"

"About John Kirby."

"About the fact that you weren't with him at Clear Lake?"

"You *know* that?"

"Oh, sure," Salter said. "You were visiting your aunt in Dauphin. So why are you telling me now?"

"Well, because . . ." She stopped.

"Because you don't mind covering up a dirty weekend, but you've been thinking, haven't you? All right, thanks very much. How was the weekend in Dauphin, by the way? Did you have nice weather?"

"Oh, shit," she said, and hung up.

Salter laughed. Then he called Environment Canada and asked them what the weather was like in southern Manitoba that weekend, especially in Winnipeg, Clear Lake, and Dauphin, just in case.

"What's the joke?" Gatenby asked.

"I'll tell you in a minute. Now, how long are we going to have to wait for that warrant?"

It came through two hours later, when Salter was about to give up for the day. "Okay, Frank. Go to work," he said.

It took Gatenby very little time to confirm that a cash withdrawal had been made at a banking machine on Bloor Street on Saturday, the day after Nancy Cowell was murdered.

"Right," Salter said. "I don't think I've forgotten anything, but I just need one more confirmation. Come along for the ride, Frank, and I'll fill you in."

"Where to?"

"Mitcham Marketplace. Tranby is the only one who can tell me what I need to know now."

He phoned Tranby to let him know he was coming and borrowed a cruiser to bully his way through the rush-hour traffic on the Don Valley Parkway. They got to Mitcham in forty-five minutes.

Tranby was sitting at the trestle table with a fresh pot of coffee bubbling behind him. He greeted them warmly. "Vic called me," he said. "That's good news. But you never thought he did it, did you?"

"We have to suspect everybody," Salter said, shaking hands. "It's the courts who assume that you're innocent."

"What can I do for you?" Tranby asked.

"Just one question," Salter said. "What was the weather like on the night Nancy Cowell was killed?"

"I told you. It was pouring down."

"In Winnipeg?"

Tranby's cup slipped, spilling coffee down his front.

Salter said, "This is the time for me to warn you that you can have a lawyer present, because I'm charging you with the murder of Nancy Cowell."

"But I was in Winnipeg!" Tranby cried.

"No, you weren't. You flew to Toronto on Friday, using the name of your old friend, A.R. Harold."

"What are you talking about?"

"You were smart. You used cash for the ticket. But not smart enough, because you didn't have enough money to get back and you withdrew some money from a banking machine in Toronto on Saturday."

"I lost my wallet. Someone was using my credit card," Tranby said.

"I thought of that. If that's true, when the forensic people go through your stuff they won't find any evidence that you were with Nancy Cowell, will they? If it isn't, they will."

"The papers said she was raped," Tranby said.

"The papers were wrong about that. So were we, for a while."

There was a long pause. "I guess I'd better get a lawyer," Tranby said at last. "How did you get on to me?"

"You were unlucky," Salter said. "It wasn't raining in Winnipeg that night. So I just asked you again in case you had made a slip. Forgotten, like."

Tranby said, "I talked to her, sure. But I didn't touch her."

"It'll be your word against the lab boys, then," Salter said.

"I didn't mean to kill her, I mean. It was an accident."

"You might make something of that," Salter conceded judicially. "You did hit her once before, of course. Gave her a black eye."

"Who told you that?"

"It came out in the investigation. Why did you hit her?"

"She turned me down. I'd seen those letters in her apartment. I knew what she wanted, and I just wanted to give her a bit of comfort. She told me to get lost. She was *advertising*, for God's sake, but I wasn't good enough for her."

"So when Kowalczyk told you he was going to see his wife, you got scared she would tell him about it."

"It would have finished me with Vic. I'd have lost this whole deal."

"So you went back to Toronto, hung around until her date left, wheedled your way in with some excuse about a message from her husband, and killed her."

"I just wanted her to promise to shut up, but she wouldn't. All she had to do was promise."

Now Salter had enough. Even Tannenbaum would have a problem with Tranby's defense. "Let's go," he said. "Put him in the car, Frank."

"Okay," Wycke said. "So tell us. Did you finger him from the start?"

"Oh, no," Salter said. "At first I was wondering about the husband. I didn't want to, because I liked the guy, but I've made that mistake before. It had to be someone with a good motive, or none at all. But it was because I was worried about Kowalczyk that I checked his story so hard. There was just time to do it—if he planned it carefully, and I think Tranby filled him with enough poison about his wife when they had lunch. I could see him flying down to Toronto and killing her as soon as he laid hands on her—just. But I couldn't see him planning it and covering his tracks. Then the guy who stole the canoe cleared him."

"Then you knew it was Tranby. Right?"

Salter shook his head. "Then I wondered about that book salesman, even Kowalczyk's sister. She was covering for him, for old times' sake. She thought he'd been caught out again with someone else's wife."

Marinelli said, "How did you know that Tranby was the one who punched her out?" He stayed some feet away from the rest of the group, unhappy about Salter's triumph.

"She told her pals she ran into a lump of iron. Engineers wear iron rings, some of them. Did you know that? Kowalczyk wears one. So does Tranby, but I didn't notice that at first."

"And the motive?" Orliff asked.

"Tranby saw some of the letters that Nancy Cowell had got back when he was in her apartment once. He assumed that she was horny, and he offered himself. When she turned him down, he got insulted. Two months later when his old friend offered him some money *and* told him he was getting back with his wife maybe, Tranby got frightened that Kowalczyk would cut him off if his wife told him what Tranby had tried. He would have, too."

"What did you need Henning's story for?" Marinelli asked.

"When a woman is killed after sexual activity, and you suspect a guy with a vasectomy, or a jealous husband, or maybe another woman, then you need another guy as well," Salter said patiently.

There was a long pause. "What gave you the lead on Tranby? I mean, when did you first see him as the possibility?"

"Something my first wife found out, that you guys had already told me, but it didn't register until I remembered what Tranby had said."

"The 'lump of iron' thing?"

"No. I was pleased with that, but it was just cute. No, she said that Loomis had told her that Cowell's actual words on the phone were, 'We got soaked coming home.' At the time I thought the big words were 'we' and 'home.' Then Tranby said it was raining too, and it wasn't until the guy who stole Kowalczyk's canoe said it was a nice night in Rat Portage that all this weather stuff started to come together. When I remembered that Adela Cowell told me at first that she went swimming with Kirby at midnight, I checked the weather bureau. Tranby was lying."

Everyone waited for someone to speak. After a few

minutes, Wycke said, "Nice work, Charlie. Now what? You going to see it through?"

Salter looked at Orliff, who shook his head. "No, you can have it, Harry. I just got lucky, and I had an advantage—my ex-wife. And if it had been raining that night in Winnipeg I'd probably still be trying to break down Kowalczyk."

"That's right," Orliff said. "It's your case. Now all you have to worry about is Tannenbaum. Have fun, boys."

"We get the credit?" Marinelli asked.

Sure, thought Salter. Orliff knows, and that's all I care. "And the work," he said.

Marinelli said, "I'll tell you one thing for sure. What with credit cards, banking machines, and Christ knows what next, you can track the whole fucking world down sitting at a computer terminal. I'm going to keep five hundred bucks in old bills under my bed in case I want to do anything illegal."

Gatenby spoke for the first time. "Don't worry. They'll invent a credit card soon that beeps if anyone looks at your bank statement."

Orliff said, "If they do, it'll be good for about three months until someone figures out how to bypass it."

"Someone like us, you mean?" Wycke said.

On that note, they broke up.

Two days before Christmas, Salter took Gerry for lunch in the ninth-floor restaurant of Simpson's, a downtown department store that serves the kind of food elderly stockbrokers enjoy in the ambience of their youth.

"I guess Nancy Cowell didn't have it coming to her after all, did she?" Gerry asked.

"Of course she didn't. She was Tranby's victim, that's all."

"Nothing to do with her life-style?"

Salter drank some coffee and wondered what it was now. "Tranby thought she was an easy proposition and got mad when he found out she wasn't. It's one of the oldest stories in the world. It wasn't her fault."

"What if it was?"

"Her fault? What do you mean?"

"There's a girl in our office. If she got killed and you started checking up on her, you might come up with ten guys she's slept with in the last month, depending on the month. She talks about it the way people we knew thirty years ago talked about dancing—you know?—out dancing every night. She goes out every single night except Sunday and she often ends up in bed. She has regular boyfriends, and they last anywhere from a month to a year, but she still goes out dancing. She has an arrangement with the guy in the flat above her—she lives in one of those converted houses—if both of them happen to be home in the evening, they usually have coffee and make love before they go to sleep. For her it's as natural as breathing. She doesn't have any morals as far as sex is concerned."

"It sounds like it."

"Let me go on. She's got plenty of morals in every other area. She's honest, kind, a great friend in need, give you the shirt off her back—all that stuff."

"The tart with the heart of gold?"

"She isn't a tart. She doesn't stand around Yonge and Dundas wearing fluorescent makeup. No one pays her. But she's got a heart of gold, all right."

"So?"

"If Nancy Cowell had checked out like that, would you have worked so hard on the case? You did make up your mind pretty early that she was probably a 'nice' girl, didn't you?"

"Yeah. She was."

"But what if she wasn't?"

"Then it would have been bloody hopeless from the start, or Homicide would have had it solved by then. But we never caught Jack the Ripper."

"And she'd have deserved it, wouldn't she?"

"She'd have brought it on herself, wouldn't she?"

"No, she wouldn't. But what's that got to do with it? She's still dead. Entitled to police protection and all that?" Gerry was not quarreling, but pleading, pleading with this man she liked.

Salter tipped the dregs of his coffee into his mouth before he replied. "This girl from the office. Did you make her up?"

"No."

Salter shrugged. "Tell her to be careful. Sooner or later she's bound to come up against a weirdo."

"That's funny. We talked about that while I was telling her about Nancy Cowell. It was okay to talk about it, wasn't it?"

"Sure. You started this whole thing."

"Yes. Well, Jackie—the girl in the office—says she can tell the weirdos a mile away. She wouldn't let one of them get close."

"There's no problem then, is there? When a girl gets killed by a weirdo, she's a nice girl by definition. I'll explain it to Homicide."

"Don't be flip, Charlie. But isn't it true? If Jackie got killed, wouldn't you say she had it coming?"

"It wouldn't matter what I thought. I'm not in Homicide. But okay, yeah, I think that would be the response. Even the compensation board says that prostitutes take the risk and therefore aren't entitled to compensation."

"But if she wasn't a prostitute?" Gerry's voice was pleading again.

Salter picked up the check. "You've made your point. Now I have to go."

She leaned back in her chair and looked at him for a long time. "I guess you're doing your best," she said finally.

Salter didn't reply, just waited for her to stand up. They made their way downstairs and out onto Richmond Street. Salter put out his hand. "Merry Christmas, Gerry," he said.

She pulled him close to her. "Merry Christmas, Charlie. Give my best to Annie." She kissed him on the lips and hugged him. Then she turned west, back to City Hall.

On December 24, Salter was attending to his desk as the smell of Christmas grew stronger. At four o'clock the smell was overpowering, and he stopped trying to work and planned his last act before going home. He waited until Gatenby left his office on an errand and then put the Swiss army knife on the sergeant's desk. When Gatenby returned, gaped, unwrapped his gift, and turned to his boss, Salter said, "It's from Annie. To thank you for all the service this year, taking messages and stuff like that. She gave one to the mailman and the garbageman, too."

But Gatenby was not fooled. "That's terrific," he said, pulling out the nail scissors and clicking them ceremonially. Then he opened a drawer in the filing cabinet and pulled out a large box, which he presented formally to Salter.

"What the hell's this, Frank?" Salter asked. "Close the door or they'll be talking about us." He opened the box and there, in a wreath of green electric cord, was a set of white outdoor Christmas lights.

"Where did you find these?"

"Downstairs," Gatenby said, shaking with glee. "The hardware store in the next block."

"The one we pass every day? Jesus Christ." There was only one thing left to say. "Merry Christmas, Frank," he said, and left.

. . .

The rest of the holiday went well, too. That evening, eight of them had a jolly time at Ed's Warehouse. There was a breath-catching moment when Salter's father insisted on ordering a third bottle of *vina di tavola*, and Annie's mother murmured something about "another beaker full of the warm South" and hoped they wouldn't all sink Lethe-ward, like a man at a neighboring table who had just fallen off his chair. But Salter's father, glistening with food and drink and his success as a host, took it as a compliment. Afterward they separated to drive home, and Salter had the pleasure of watching Annie very nearly walk past the lighted tree in front of the house before she saw what he had arranged, with the help of a neighbor, to greet her. She was overcome, and they watched *A Christmas Carol* in a circle of grins, chanting the lines along with the actors.

The next morning Annie went properly mad over the little silver tray, and the boys were delighted as puppies with their gifts. From them Salter got a combined gift, a deluxe Swiss army knife, and from Annie he got a squash racquet of a kind he had coveted but been too cheap to buy for himself, and an envelope. Inside, in fake legal language, was a statement that Charles Salter now owned the rights to one weekend of his choice at Wycke's cottage every year in perpetuity.

"What's this?" Salter asked.

"It's called 'Time Sharing,' " Annie said. "I bought one weekend's fishing for you from Harry Wycke. He didn't charge much. I was going to put it in your stocking."

"That's terrific," Salter said. "Will you come?"

"We'll all come," Annie said. "For one weekend."

"As long as I don't have to fish," Angus said.

"You could use your knife to clean the fish," Seth pointed out and was slightly surprised when Salter embraced him and tried to throw him up to the ceiling, as he used to when Seth was a lot smaller.

They ate a brunch of smoked salmon and scrambled eggs and moved through a not-too-long afternoon to turkey and paper hats, and by keeping everything well oiled Salter took them smoothly through to the evening, when a tiny miracle happened. Annie had brought a small piano into their marriage on which she occasionally practiced her childhood accomplishments, but it was there mainly to interest the boys in taking lessons, an enterprise that had never got off the ground. At one point Annie's mother moved to the instrument and played some carols, which they all tried to sing. This ceremony out of the way, Salter's father asked her if she knew the tune to "She Was Only a Bird in a Gilded Cage," a song he had learned from *his* father. Not only did she know it, she also knew every other song he mentioned because, it transpired, English music-hall songs had once been a hobby of hers, and her memory for them was as retentive as it was for scraps of verse. Thus Salter watched and listened in wonder to a side of his father he had forgotten about as the old man, transported with pleasure, rumbled his way hoarsely through a dozen favorites. Even the boys enjoyed him, especially in a number called "Oh, Nicholas, Don't Be So Ridiculous," though the favorite by consensus was "When It's Twilight in Italy, It's Wednesday Over Here."

It was the best Christmas ever, the boys said. On Boxing Day they prepared themselves for the surprise promised by Annie's father, a surprise that turned out to be both banal and ideal—an early dinner in the revolving restaurant on top of the CN tower, the tallest structure in the commonwealth.

"Have you ever eaten here?" Annie's father asked the company. No one had. "I thought not," he said. "I've never met anyone who lives in Toronto who has. Now you have."

It suited everybody perfectly, for different reasons. Even Salter's father felt totally at home, as he confided to Salter later, once he realized that it cost no more than his own treat, and, in his opinion, the food at Ed's Warehouse was better.

"And I should have warned him not to order house wine," he said authoritatively. "I had that a few weeks ago when May took me out for my birthday to a fancy restaurant on the Danforth. It's piss."

That night Salter brushed Christmas off his teeth and slid in beside his wife. "I think we made it," he said. "Want to celebrate?"

About the Author

ERIC WRIGHT was born in England but emigrated to Canada as a young man. For some years he has lived in Toronto, where he is a teacher. Married, with two daughters, he has written for television, and his "Blitzkrieg Days" was published in *The New Yorker*. His first Charlie Salter mystery, *The Night the Gods Smiled,* won the John Creasey Award in Britain for Best First Mystery of the Year. He is the author also of *Smoke Detector* and *Death in the Old Country*.

9.00
JAN